THE MONKEY'S HAIRCUT
and Other Stories Told by the Maya

THE MONKEY'S HAIRCUT

AND OTHER STORIES TOLD BY THE MAYA

Edited by John Bierhorst

86-87
"221"

Illustrated by Robert Andrew Parker

William Morrow and Company · New York

Printed in the United States of America
Designed by Jane Byers Bierhorst
1 2 3 4 5 6 7 8 9 10

Library of Congress Cataloging-in-Publication Data

Bierhorst, John.
The monkey's haircut, and other stories told by the Maya.

Bibliography: p.
Summary: A Collection of twenty-two traditional tales from the Mayas,
including "How Christ Was Chased" and "The Corn in the Rock."
1. Mayas—Legends. [1. Mayas—Legends. 2. Indians
of Central America—Legends]
I. Parker, Robert Andrew, ill. II. Title.
F1435.3.F6B53 1986 398.2'097281 [398.2] 85-28471
ISBN 0-688-04269-4

Acknowledgment is made for permission to adapt or translate from the
following publications (for further details, see Notes on Sources and Variants):
Marianna C. Slocum, "The Origin of Corn and Other Tzeltal Myths," *Tlalocan*,
vol. 5 (1965), pp. 1–45; Diego de Diego Antonio and Karen Dakin,
"El conejo y la coyota," *Tlalocan*, vol. 9 (1982), pp. 161–72;
John G. Fought, *Chorti (Mayan) Texts 1*, University of Pennsylvania Press,
1972; Robert D. Bruce, *El libro de Chan K'in*, Colección Científica (lingüística),
no. 12, Instituto Nacional de Antropología e Historia (Mexico), 1974.

Contents

THE MONKEY'S HAIRCUT
and Other Stories Told by the Maya

Introduction

I am doing it, and you are doing it. Can you guess what it is?

"Breathing" is the answer to this Maya riddle, collected fifty years ago near the ruins of Chichén Itzá. Here is another, from the same region, recorded in the eighteenth century: Son, have you seen the green water holes in the rock? There are two of them, a cross is raised between them. Answer: They are a man's eyes.

Although native American riddles have been collected as far north as Alaska and as far south as Chile, it is fair to say that the Maya Indians, who live in Guatemala and southeastern Mexico, are the champion riddlers of the New World. Theirs is a society that has always placed great value on cleverness.

During the early Middle Ages, when Europe was still struggling with Roman numerals, the Maya were using a number system that included zeros, permitting swift, accurate calculation. This we know from inscriptions in stone. From the few bark-paper books that have survived we know that Maya astronomers were able to predict the movements of the moon and the planet Venus.

Among the many humbler examples of Maya ingenuity is one that did not come to light until 1984. In that year, archaeologists excavating a tomb in Guatemala discovered a jar with a lid that could not be pulled loose. Then, by accident, they found that it came off by twisting. Before this, it had not been known that the ancient Maya had screw-top lids.

Today the Maya spirit of inventiveness finds expression in word games, puns, and exchanges of wit. Double meanings are much appreciated, not only in riddles but in everyday conversation and, often, in storytelling. Unfortunately, it is seldom possible to translate this kind of humor. Wordplays in the story How Christ Was Chased are lost in English. Nevertheless, the whimsical character of the bird calls in this tale and in the closing phrases of The Miser's Jar can be sensed even in translation.

More obvious is the double meaning in Rabbit and Coyote, which enables Rabbit to dupe Coyote and escape from his cage. In Tup and the Ants, the plot of the story actually hinges on a pun: the old man says, "Cut trees," which Tup interprets to mean "clear the forest," while his foolish brothers waste time cutting into trees, trying to hollow them out.

What the reader of Maya stories should keep in mind is that the element of wit is never entirely absent. Even the most ancient myth, even the most serious tale, has its not so serious moments.

Divisions of the Maya

It is common to think of the Maya as a people who built what many believe to have been the most brilliant civilization in the western hemisphere. During their classic period, which lasted from about A.D. 200 to 800, the Maya perfected the arts of painting, sculpture, and architecture and developed a system of writing. Palaces and pyramids at such sites as Tikal in Guatemala and Uxmal in Yucatan bear witness to a culture of great competence and refinement.

What is less fully appreciated is that many features of the ancient culture have survived into the twentieth century. The Maya today are as numerous, or nearly so, as they were a thousand years ago. And today, as then, they are a diverse people, practicing local customs within an overall pattern that is recognizably Maya.

Like the nations of Western Europe, the Maya speak not one language but a group of related languages. According to a well-known theory, the two million Maya speakers of today are all descended from a tribe that lived in the mountains of western Guatemala some four thousand years ago. Over the centuries small groups broke away, and gradually each developed its own way of speaking.

The Yucatec were among the first to leave, migrating northward. Eventually they settled the entire Yucatan Peninsula and built the great cities of Uxmal and Chichén Itzá. The land that the Yucatec found waiting for them was a warm, pleasantly dry country—as it is today. There are almost no rivers but many sinkholes and grottoes partially filled with ground water. Such a watering place figures prominently in the Yucatec tale called The Bird Bride. This story, like many modern stories from the region, shows the influence of European fairy tales.

Since their language is similar to Yucatec, the Lacandon Maya, who live across the border from Guatemala in the Mexican state of Chiapas, must have begun their migration at about the same time. Unlike the Yucatec, however, the Lacandon have preserved a truly ancient way of life, still using bark cloth and dugout canoes. Many of their stories show no European influence whatsoever. One, The Mole Catcher, is included in this collection.

A little farther south, in the Chiapas high country, are the towns of the Tzotzil and the Tzeltal. On close inspection, however, the towns prove to be nearly vacant, the people themselves living mostly in hamlets scattered over the countryside. The towns are in fact ceremonial centers, filling up whenever there is a market day or a religious celebration. In the past twenty-five years a great many Tzotzil and Tzeltal stories have been collected, mostly with tape recorders, enabling translators to produce English versions of considerable freshness and accuracy.

By far the greatest number of Maya groups still live in the highlands of western Guatemala. These include the Cakchiquel, Ixil, Kanhobal, Mam, Quiche, and Tzutuhil. Storytelling traditions in the highlands vary from valley to valley, but in general this region seems to have preserved more of the ancient myths than any other. In eastern Guatemala, at somewhat lower elevations, live the Chorti and the Kekchi. Although story collecting among the Maya did not really get under way until the 1930s, many Kekchi tales were already known from collections that had been made as early as the turn of the century. The earliest recorded stories in this book, therefore, are from the Kekchi of eastern Guatemala and adjacent parts of southern Belize.

Home and community

Maya people today are still using the traditional Maya house, a one-story one-room structure with a rectangular ground plan and a door in the middle of one of the long sides. The roof is a picturesque high-peaked thatch with plenty of space inside for the storage loft often mentioned in Maya folktales as an excellent hiding place. Though it varies from region to region, the basic design has not changed in a thousand years, as we know from the houses shown in reliefs and murals at Uxmal and Chichén Itzá.

Inside, at one end, is the sleeping area, furnished today with hammocks or a modern mattress, though at one time the Maya probably slept on cots made of poles lashed together, as the Lacandon have continued to do. Opposite is the kitchen area, where foods derived from corn are routinely prepared each day. Of these the tortilla is basic, usually flavored with ground chili peppers and supplemented by a thin cornmeal beverage called atole. Corn paste, another staple, is often taken by men to the fields, where they mix it with water to make corn soup, or pozole. Meats, including deer, paca, peccary, and even chicken, are luxuries in most regions, as are chocolate, honey, and such fruits as sapodilla and watermelon. All of these are mentioned in folktales.

Ordinarily the house is occupied by a married couple and their several children. In some regions, notably Yucatan and Chiapas, a bridegroom is expected to stay in his wife's house and work for her father for a few weeks or perhaps as long as a year or two. After this period of "bride service," he and his wife go to live with his parents until they are able to build a house of their own. Maya listeners will understand that the hero of Tup and the Ants is performing bride service. The same is true of the hero of The Mole

Catcher, who must work for his father-in-law, the dreaded Death Maker.

In day-to-day living, each family fends for itself. Extended family groups, or clans, are unimportant or entirely lacking. Yet the family does establish ties with the surrounding community through a kind of ritual kinship between married couples. The couples rely upon each other, calling each other "compadres" (coparents). In most cases a man's compadre (cofather) is the godparent of his child. The wife of the compadre is addressed as "comadre" (comother).

With considerable formality, the father of a newborn child pays a visit to the couple he has selected to be godparents, bringing them gifts. Among the Tzotzil the new father may say to the couple, "Won't you be so kind as to let me borrow your feet and your hands, to sustain for me the soul of God's angel [meaning the child]?"

At first the couple must politely refuse. The man may say, "Ah, could it be true, son? But won't you look for someone else? Isn't there somebody else you would rather have? There are always other men and women."

The father persists: "No, it's you I decided on, sir. Won't you do me the favor of embracing my child?"

The couple finally consents: "God's angel can't be refused." Eventually the man will add—using the all-important word: "All right, so that's the way it is. We will become compadres." The father replies, "Ah, all right, compadre."

The relationship is not one to be taken lightly. In the story called The Bad Compadre we learn what happens to a man who betrays the trust that has been placed in him.

The cornfield

The Maya practice what is sometimes called slash-and-burn agriculture. Before a field can be cultivated, trees and brush must be cleared away, then burned to ashes. The next year the same field can be used again, but by the third year the soil may be worn out. If so, a new field must be carved out of the forest.

This is grueling work. But making it into a religious duty helps the men to endure it more easily. Special prayers are recited for each stage of the job, ceremonies are held, sacrificial offerings of food are brought to the field, and the corn itself is addressed by such mystical names as "divine grace" or "Our Lord's sunbeams."

For the storyteller, however, the answer is simply to imagine that the work can be done by magic, usually in one night (Tup and the Ants, Rosalie, The Bad Compadre), or to wonder what would happen if the task were avoided altogether (Buzzard Man).

In reality, the job takes many months, beginning with a careful measuring of the land to be cleared. For the Yucatec farmer the unit is the cord, or mecate, an area about sixty feet square. On the average, one man can cultivate seventy-five mecates in a year, roughly one acre. So we can appreciate the cruelty of the father-in-law in the story Rosalie, who demands that a cornfield of one hundred mecates be made in one day.

To add to the labor, good land is not always available near home. In search of soil fertile enough to yield a crop, the farmer may have to travel miles through the forest. This explains why the farmer's sons in the tale The Bird Bride take so long to get to the field, even stopping for a nap at the halfway point.

In the northern and western parts of Yucatan some Maya men hire themselves out to work on plantations where henequen, a kind of maguey or century plant, is grown for its fiber, used in making rope. Similarly, some men work on the large coffee plantations in the Guatemala highlands. These plantations are operated not by Maya but by well-to-do landowners of European descent.

Gods and demons

There is not a single Maya settlement, even in the remote country of the Lacandon, that has not been touched by Christianity. In fact, the Maya as a whole are Christian and have been so, at least in name, since the arrival of Spanish missionaries in the mid-1500s.

Yet in the twentieth century the Kekchi Maya have continued to address prayers to the Lord of the Hills and the Valleys, also called Lord of the Thirteen Hills. The people of Yucatan have not abandoned the old rain god, Chac (who has a frog orchestra, since frogs, when they croak, are thought to be calling for rain). And, not surprisingly, the Lacandon have kept up an elaborate mythology explaining the origins and activities of various gods.

According to the most recent information, obtained in the 1970s, there is a major Lacandon deity known as Hachakyum, also called Our Lord. Hachakyum made the sun, but his elder brother, Sukunkyum, is the one who carries it through the sky each day. At night Sukunkyum goes to his house in the underworld, feeds the sun, and spends time with his wife until the sun has to be brought up to the sky again. Naturally, when it is dark on the earth, it is light in the underworld, and vice versa.

Another of the gods, one who lives in the underworld permanently, is Kisin (Death Maker). Some Lacandon have identified Death Maker with the devil of Christianity. But the idea of an underworld ruler of the dead is a traditional Maya concept, illustrated in paintings that are more than a thousand years old.

Of secondary importance in Lacandon myths, the sun god plays a major role in stories of other Maya regions, where his adventures are said to have taken place in the days when he still lived on the earth. Two stories in particular have been widely told. In one, the sun takes a bride, who becomes the moon. In the other, he is a little boy who lives with his grandmother. After getting rid of his cruel brother and, usually, bringing about the origin of animals, the boy rises to the sky and becomes the sun, while his grandmother, at least in some versions, becomes the moon.

The story Blue Sun has been included in this book as an example of the second type of sun myth. In this version the hero's cruel brother is called Blue Sun (perhaps a better translation would be Green Sun, or First Sun), and the hero himself presumably becomes the sun we see today.

The trickster Rabbit is another important figure in Maya stories, though it is not known whether he belongs to the old Maya mythology. Rabbit tales in recent years have been among the most popular of all Maya folktales, told everywhere, even in the Lacandon region. But these, for the most part, are the familiar Br'er Rabbit stories, including the most famous of all, The Tar Baby, in which the hero becomes stuck to a lifelike doll made of tar or wax. Such stories were evidently imported from Spain or perhaps Africa. Yet rabbits with human attributes and trickster-like personalities can be seen in paintings on ancient Maya jars.

In modern Yucatan the trickster is called Juan Tul (John Rabbit), and it has been said that he is a tall thin man with a long moustache and lots of whiskers.

Demons, monsters, and witches add a gruesome element to Maya folklore, but they are seldom the subject of full-fledged stories. For example, a person may say that "not long ago" his "cousin" saw a xtabay (pronounced shta-BYE, a phantom woman who lures people to their death) and was so frightened he ran all the way home. Such reports belong to the realm of hearsay or rumor. Two unusually well developed witch stories, however, appear in the present collection, the Tzotzil story of the Charcoal Cruncher and the little Kekchi tale entitled How a Witch Escaped.

The art of storytelling

Most Maya storytellers make a distinction between myths and other kinds of stories. Myths take place in an ancient time before the world was as it is today. They explain such things as how the moon came to be and how the woodpecker got its red crest. As defined by a Cakchiquel storyteller, a tale of this kind is called an ejemplo, a tale that explains things. The term is also used in Yucatan, but with a broader meaning. The Yucatec ejemplo may be an origin myth, a story about Christ, or any tale with a moral. An ordinary folktale or fairy tale, on the other hand, is called a cuento.

Story categories are not rigid, and it is often impossible to say whether a tale is an ejemplo or a cuento. In fact, the definition may vary from storyteller to storyteller.

Probably the most usual occasions for telling stories are men's gatherings, especially work breaks when men are away from home. But Margaret Redfield, wife of the anthropologist Robert Redfield, was able to obtain many Yucatec stories from women and found that tales had been handed down from mother to daughter. One woman recalled that when she was a girl, she and her mother would get into their hammocks at night. Then, after reciting a prayer, the mother would tell cuentos.

There are no fixed rules for opening or closing a story. But it will be noticed that many narrators like to begin by announcing that this is a tale of the ancient time or a story told by the ancestors. Even a trivial Rabbit tale, hardly a myth, can begin in the grand manner: "A story of the ancestors, long ago."

When finishing, some narrators like to add a personal touch. For instance, many of the Yucatec tales collected by the linguist Manuel Andrade in the 1930s end with a comment that continues the story line, as if to say, "I saw it with my own eyes." The Monkey's Haircut is one of these; and notice that the Chorti tale Toad and Hawk ends with a similar observation: "If I had been there, I would have caught him in my hat [referring to Toad, who fell from the sky]."

Occasionally a storyteller will slip into a singsong of paired phrases. It does not happen often, yet it is frequent enough and distinctive enough to be called a Maya trait. The best example in this book is The Bad Compadre. After a paragraph or two the reader begins to realize that something is different. If certain passages are rewritten as poetry, it is easier to see how one phrase is balanced by another phrase. Here is the beginning of the second paragraph:

> His compadre, Juan, heard about it.
>   Then Juan said to his wife,
> "Do me a favor,
>   do me an errand.
> Go see our compadre,
>   maybe talk to his wife."
> The woman went,
>   she talked to the man.

Here is the entire sixth paragraph of the Lacandon story The Mole Catcher:

> The daughter of Death Maker went in first.
>   The mole catcher went after her.
> Inside he managed to find the path,
>   although it was very dark.
> After he had walked a short distance,
>   he came into the light again.
> When he had walked ten paces,
>   a brightness appeared.
> The sun had come out.
>   "It's dawn!" he said.

Only in tales that have been carefully translated from one of the Maya languages is it possible to detect this feature. It does not show up in the many stories that have been freely translated or that have been taken down in Spanish through an interpreter.

In all, roughly a thousand Maya tales have been recorded since 1900. Yet this book includes only twenty-two. The reason is partly that many are variants, partly that many are incomplete or poorly told. To show how variants may differ, two versions of the so-called Chac story have here been included, the second of which, less fully told, is called The Lord of the Clouds.

Of the stories most widely reported, How Christ Was Chased ranks first in popularity, followed closely by the linked incidents in Rabbit and Coyote and in Rabbit and Puma. The Corn in the Rock comes next, followed by Lord Sun's Bride and, finally, Blue Sun. No book of Maya stories would be complete without these.

Maya adaptations of European fairy tales form an important secondary element, here represented by The Bird Bride, The Miser's Jar, Rosalie, and The Lost Children. For readers of English the best known of these is the last, which resembles Hansel and Gretel and is even closer to the French fairy tale Hop-o'-My-Thumb. Cinderella and Ali Baba and the Forty Thieves have been reported from both Guatemala and Yucatan, but the available versions are not well told and have been excluded for that reason.

The *Popol Vuh*

Although Maya stories were not collected before 1900, there exists a remarkable sixteenth-century document in which the stories are woven together in a lengthy origin legend, almost like a novel. This is the well-known *Popol Vuh* (Council Book). Written in the language of the Quiche Maya, the *Popol Vuh* was discovered in the Guatemala highlands about 1700 and became a subject of serious scholarship beginning in the late 1800s. Today it can be compared with modern folktales to show that recently collected stories hark back to traditions at least four hundred years old.

The story of the young hero, the future sun, who lives with his grandmother is related in several chapters of the *Popol Vuh*. In the old Quiche version, however, the hero has a twin, and it is the twin, not the grandmother, who becomes the moon.

In an earlier chapter it is told how the twin heroes' mother finds her husband in the underworld. He has been murdered in a previous episode and appears to her only as a death's-head, which she nevertheless accepts. One is reminded of the Lacandon mole catcher, whose underworld bride reveals her naked skull. He, too, accepts this without question. Evidently the mysterious theme of love and death has a long tradition in the oral literature of the Maya.

The twins themselves, after they have left their grandmother, travel to the underworld, where the lords of death subject them to a series of trials. In one of these the lords have the twins imprisoned and give them each a lighted cigar, which must be kept burning all night. In the dark the twins fool the prison guards by attaching fireflies to the ends of the unlit cigars.

Almost the same story was still being told in the twentieth century, with Jesus as the imprisoned smoker (see How Christ Was Chased). Very likely the tale is much older than the *Popol Vuh* and evidently goes back at least a thousand years. In an underworld scene painted on an ancient Maya jar the firefly is shown holding the lighted cigar. This art object is probably from northern Guatemala and has been dated between A.D. 600 and 900.

A true story

Stories, in the sense that the term is here understood, create a world that could hardly be put together out of actual experience, even though the narrator may insist the story is true, as folk narrators often do. In view of this apparent contradiction, it helps to ask what "true" really means.

The Maya do, of course, tell things that have happened to themselves or to people they know. Such unremarkable, "true" tales do not belong in storybooks. Nevertheless, it may be of interest to take a look at one of these real-life accounts to see how it compares with what we consider fiction.

The following story was told to Manuel Andrade, who later had the opportunity to verify it but had to promise he would withhold the names of the people involved in order to protect their privacy. The story was narrated by Bernardino Tun, a Yucatec man, who said it had happened to a friend of his while courting the girl he eventually married.

When the boy began visiting the girl, she definitely said she would marry him. So the boy bought brandy and cigarettes and gave them to his mother to bring to the girl's father. The mother went at dusk.

When she arrived, she gave the gifts to the father and they talked for a while. The mother mentioned why she had come. "I know nothing about it," said the father. "Come back in fifteen days and I will tell you what there is."

When the fifteen days were up, the boy bought more brandy and the mother again took it to the girl's father. But the father said, "If you are here on the business that you began, madam, there is absolutely nothing favorable. I am not going to marry my daughter to anyone."

Later, however, the girl repeated her promise to the boy. "When I say something, it is final," she said. Then they grasped each other's hand, and the boy told her he would return for her within fifteen days.

The boy went away to another village. When he came back, the girl's mother, who had become suspicious, was watching her closely. A day passed, and another day. On the third day the boy saw the girl going to bathe, and he said to her, "If we are to go, we should go at once."

"My mother has gone to my sister's to take her some food," said the girl. "Let us go before she returns." The boy led her to the house of his brother, who lived nearby, and went out again by himself. When he got to the village square, he found that everyone was looking for the stolen girl. Her father had complained to the commissioner.

Ten men were ordered to guard the roads leading from the village. Hearing this, the boy returned to his brother's house and said to the girl, "You are being looked for by your father. They have blocked the roads. But we can get past them."

At midnight he said, "Well, let us go. The moon is shining brightly." They went and made their way around the place where the men were stationed, walking on until they got to the village where the boy was now living. Meanwhile the poor guards spent the whole night watching. They saw no one.

When the girl's father heard that the young couple had not been caught, he paid ten men to go look for them in the boy's new village. The next day the boy was called in by his village commissioner, and there were the ten men, standing around with guns. The boy explained that he had not stolen the girl. "She came of her own will," he said. The commissioner believed him and sent the men home.

On the way back the men got lost. For three days they were arriving one by one, and all this time the girl's father was paying them ten pesos a day.

The father then went to a higher commissioner, and the government gave orders to have the boy arrested. But when the boy went before the high commissioner, he offered to pay him a hundred pesos if he would let him go free. The commissioner said that would be all right, and the boy went home. He remained with the girl, and both were very happy.

Time passed, and one day the boy said, "I am going to visit my old village to see my brothers." The next morning he set out. When he had arrived at his brother's house, he bathed, then went out for a walk. While walking, he met the man who was now his father-in-law.

"How is my daughter over there?" said the poor man.

"What do you mean by asking me about her now?" said the boy. At this the father began to cry. When he saw that the father was crying, he said to him, "Do not cry, Papá. She is well. I will bring her to visit you."

"Forget the things that have happened to us," said the father, "and I also will forget them." After a while the boy brought his wife. When they arrived, the parents were very happy to see them. They gave them caresses without end.

Though true, such a story is not likely to have been told beyond the next village. And by now, some fifty years after Andrade heard it, it presumably has been forgotten. Yet it is similar to at least two of the stories in this book, tales that have traveled hundreds or even thousands of miles and that have lasted for generations.

One of these is Lord Sun's Bride. The eloping couple, the deceived father, and even the possibility of the father's repentance are all there. The same situation, exaggerated by the most fantastic details, is the subject of the story called Rosalie. We meet the deceived father again in The Mole Catcher, and once again in Rabbit Gets Married. These are stories that are true for people beyond the confines of a single village or a single time.

In the preceding pages I have tried to be helpful by explaining what a Maya house looks like, what foods are eaten, how a cornfield is planted, and what gods are worshipped—as well as what troubles a young man may have with his bride's parents. But in the end, these details are transformed by the storyteller's art. The world that he, or she, creates is a world of fantasy. Yet it exists everywhere, within and beyond the territory of the Maya. This is a world, unreal as it may be, that makes it possible to find what is true for each of us.

J.B.

The Bird Bride

A farmer, who had three sons, saw that his cornfield was being eaten up little by little. But he could never catch a glimpse of whatever it was that did the damage.

Finally he said to his sons, "The one who can bring this creature to me, dead or alive, will inherit my land and everything I have."

The youngest promised to go at once. But his two brothers mocked him. "How could a stupid boy like you do anything?" they cried.

"The older boys must try first," said the father.

So the oldest of the three took his father's finest shotgun and a big pack-lunch and set out when the moon was full. Halfway to the cornfield, already a little tired, he stopped at the edge of a water hole, where a toad was croaking.

"You pest! Don't you ever sleep?" he said. "How can I take a rest with you croaking like this?"

"Let me go with you," said the toad, "and I will tell you who is eating your corn."

"What does a toad know?" said the young man, and he picked it up and threw it into the water.

When he got to the cornfield, he found more damage than ever. But though he watched all night, he did not see the creature itself. Furious, he returned to the house.

"What happened?" asked the father. The son could tell him no more than that he had sat up all night waiting for the thief, but it had not come back. The old man said, "You lose. You will not be my heir."

It was now the second eldest's turn. He took a shotgun and a bag with some food, and off he went. Halfway down the trail, he, too, met the toad, croaking at the water hole.

"Shut up, toad," he said. "I want to take a nap."

"Let me go with you," replied the toad. "I will help you."

"I don't need help," said the young man, and he fell

asleep. Offended, the toad stole the corn paste out of the pack-lunch. When the young man woke up and saw that the food was missing, he threw the toad into the water and went on his way.

When he got to the cornfield, he saw a beautiful bird rising into the air. He aimed his shotgun and fired. But only a few feathers dropped to the ground. Nevertheless, he picked up the feathers and ran home.

As soon as he saw his father and brothers, he laughed and said, "I have caught the cornfield thief. Look, here are its feathers."

But the youngest was not satisfied. "You have brought feathers and nothing else," he said. "I will go get the whole bird."

The youngest asked for a shotgun and a bag with only a little food in it, and off he went. When he got to the water hole and found the toad, he went up to it and said, "Little toad, I will give you half my pack-lunch if you will tell me who is ruining my cornfield. Help me, and I will take you with me always, wherever I go."

The toad was pleased and said, "Young man, I like what you say and am only sorry your brothers did not listen to me. They will be punished. But all will go well with you."

Then the toad said, "Beneath the water of this pool

there is a pebble that will grant you any wish."

"If I wanted a bride, could I get one?" asked the young man.

"Oh, not only a beautiful bride but a huge beautiful house where the two of you would live happily," replied the toad.

The boy then wished for the bride and the house and to catch the cornfield thief as well. The toad assured him his wishes would be granted, and after sharing the pack-lunch, they set out.

No sooner had they arrived at the cornfield than they saw the bird fly down and settle itself among the corn-stalks. The young man raised his gun. But just as he was about to shoot, the bird looked up and said, "Do not kill me."

Amazed, the boy said nothing. Slowly he lowered the gun. Moving closer, the creature said, "I am not what I seem. I was changed into a bird by a sorceress, because I refused to marry her evil son."

Remembering the wish he had made to the pebble, the boy realized that this must be the one who would be his bride.

"If what you say is true," he said, "come with me. Come with me and my friend the toad. We will take you home and have you changed back to the way you were. I will ask you to marry me, and I will offer you a huge beautiful house where we will live happily." The creature accepted, and he took her with him.

When he got home, his father and brothers were astounded to see him with the bird and the toad. "Here is the whole bird," he said, "not just a few feathers. She was eating our corn, but she is not to blame. She was bewitched by a sorceress who hated her for not marrying her evil son. She will be changed into a girl again because the pebble at the water hole promised me a beautiful bride, and this is she. My friend the toad has helped me to have this good luck."

He turned to the toad and said, "Let her be changed to the way she was, and let it be tomorrow that we have the huge beautiful house."

The toad croaked once, and as the bird vanished a young woman appeared in its place. She thanked the ones who had saved her and promised to be the young man's bride.

"And you have saved my cornfield," said the father to his youngest son. "You are the winner. You will be my heir."

The next morning at daybreak, there before them stood

a huge beautiful house. After they were married, the toad lived with them, croaking away in remembrance of the day it had met the good young man.

The jealous brothers wanted to harm the house and its owner, but they did not succeed and had to run away full of shame, leaving the winner rich and happy.

Yucatec

The Miser's Jar

There was once an old miser who had a beautiful jar. It was so beautiful that anyone who saw it wanted to buy it. Yet no one could meet the old man's price.

One day when he came home from his work in the cornfield, his daughter, who was grinding cornmeal, said, "Father, three people came to see the jar this morning, a gentleman, another man, and a priest."

"And what did you tell them?" asked the old man.

"I told them to come back this afternoon."

"You are a wise girl, and you have made good use of your wisdom," said the father. "When these three re-

· 32

turn, as they surely will, you must say to each one that you have decided to sell the jar for five hundred pesos without my knowledge. Tell the gentleman to come for it at eight o'clock tonight, the other man to come at half past eight, and the priest to come at nine."

The girl did as she was told, and at eight o'clock the gentleman arrived. But just as the girl had finished counting the money he had brought, there was a noise at the door of the hut, and throwing the money into one corner, she cried, "Go up into the loft! If my father finds you here, he will kill you."

While the gentleman was hurrying up to the loft, the other man came in. But before he could leave with the jar there was again a noise at the door. "Go up to the loft," cried the girl, "or my father will kill you!"

The man climbed quickly into the loft, and the priest came in. He was in a great hurry and had the jar already in his hands when the voice of the old man was heard outside. The priest trembled with fear as the girl cried, "Put the jar down and go up to the loft!"

When the girl's father came in, he asked, "Where is the gentleman's money?"

"There in the corner," she answered.

"And the other man's money?"

"There in the corner."

"And the priest's money?"

"There in the corner."

After a pause the old man asked, "And the gentleman, where is he?"

"Up in the loft."

"And the other man?"

"Up in the loft."

"And the priest?"

"Up in the loft."

"You are a wise girl," said the old man. Then he took his large carrying sack off his shoulder, put it in the middle of the floor, and set fire to it. The three men in the loft were soon dead from breathing the smoke, for the sack was full of dried chilis.

"Well," said the old man, "we still have the jar and three times five hundred pesos as well."

"But we have three dead men in the loft," replied his daughter.

"The fool will get rid of them for us tomorrow," said the old man. "In the morning I will go find him and tell him you have sent me to ask him to come have breakfast with us."

The girl knew that the fool was in love with her and

would do whatever she asked. So the next morning, when the three of them had finished their breakfast, she told the fool that she and her father were troubled because a priest who had eaten with them the night before had choked to death, and, fearful that it would be found out, they had put him in the loft, not daring to take him out for burial.

"Don't worry about a dead priest," said the fool. "Promise to marry me, and I will get rid of him without any trouble." The girl gave her promise, but no sooner had the fool set out with the dead priest on his back than she sewed a cassock and put it on the gentleman.

When the fool returned and began talking of marriage, the girl laughed and said, "Don't try to deceive me. I know very well that while I was at the stream getting water, you sneaked into the house and put the priest back in the loft."

Seeing the gentleman in the cassock, the fool said, "I buried you once and I'll bury you again." Then he set out with the gentleman on his back, and the girl sewed another cassock and put it on the last of the three dead men. And when the fool came back and said, "He'll lie where I put him this time, because I piled heavy stones on the grave," the girl frowned and said, "Why don't you tell me the truth? I know very well that while I was out getting firewood, you came in and put the priest back in the loft."

"Well, I'll bet he doesn't come back after I bury him the third time," said the fool when he saw the cassock. As soon as he had set out with the last of the dead men on his back, the girl called to her father, who was hiding nearby. He came in, filled the beautiful jar full of money, and strapped it on his back. The girl strapped the grindstone on her back, and after setting fire to the hut they began walking toward the east.

They had not gone far when the old man caught his foot in a root and, stumbling, fell into a deep pool that lay next to the road. The girl plunged in, trying to save him, but with the weight of the grindstone she sank, too, and that was the end of them both.

The fool, coming back and not finding the hut, followed the tracks of the old man and his daughter all the way to the edge of the pool. As he sat down and began to weep, he was changed into the where-where bird. And to this day the bird may be seen near pools and in wet places, crying, "Where, where? Where, where?"

Kekchi

Buzzard Man

Once there was a man long ago. He was very lazy. A loafer. He didn't want to do anything. He didn't want to work. When he went to clear trees, he asked for tortillas to take along. But he only went to eat.

Lying on his back in the woods, watching the buzzards gliding in the sky, he said, "Come on down, buzzard, come here, let's talk! Give me your suit!" The buzzard never came down.

Every day the man returned home. "How is your work?" his wife would ask.

"There is work to do, there is still work to do. There

is quite a bit because it can't be done easily. There are so many large logs," the man would say. And he left and he came back. And he left and he came back. And that's how the year passed.

The poor woman's heart! "My corn is about to be harvested," she said. But how could her corn be harvested? Sleeping is what the man did. He spreads out his woolen tunic. He goes to sleep. He makes a pillow out of his tortillas.

"God, My Lord, holy buzzard, how is it that you don't do anything at all?" he would say. "You fly, gliding easily along. You don't work. But me, it's hard with me. I'm suffering terribly. What agony I suffer! Look at my hands! They have lots of sores already. My hands hurt, so now I can't work. My hands are worn out. I don't want to work at all."

Maybe Our Lord grew tired of it. The buzzard finally came down.

"Well, what is it you want with me, talking that way?"

"It's just that you seem so well off," said the man. "Without a care you fly in the sky. Now me, I suffer so much. I suffer a lot, working in my cornfield, and I haven't any corn. I'm poor. My wife is scolding me. That's why, if you just wanted to, you could take my clothes, and I'll go buzzarding."

"Ah!" said the buzzard. "Well, I'll go first to ask permission. I'll come back, depending on what I'm told."

"Go, then!"

"Wait for me."

The man waited. He sat down, waiting for the buzzard. "Why don't you come to change places with me? I can't stand it anymore, I'm tired of working," he said. He had taken his ax and his little billhook with him to clear the land. He cleared a tiny bit. He felled two trees, then he returned home again.

"How about it, have you finished clearing your land?" asked his wife.

"Oh, it seems to be nearly ready."

"Ah," she said. And another day passed.

"So, I'm going again today," he said. "Get up, please, and make me a couple of tortillas."

"All right," said the wife, and the man went off to talk to the buzzard. He sat down immediately. "God, I'm hungry already. I have too much work."

"Oh?" said someone. It was the buzzard, coming down. It landed.

"What? What do you say?"

"Our Lord has given permission. He says we can change places. He says for you to go, and me to stay."

"But won't my wife realize that it isn't me anymore?" asked the man.

"No, she won't know. It's by Our Lord's command," said the buzzard, and he took off his feathers. He shook off all his feathers. The man took off his pants, his shirt, his wool tunic, everything. The other one put them on, and when he finished putting on the wool tunic, the clothes began to stick on. And you see, the buzzard's feathers and everything, they too began to stick on.

"See here," said the one who had been a buzzard, "don't do anything wrong. Let me tell you how we eat. We see fumes coming up when there is a dead horse, or sheep, or whatever. You'll see that if it's a small meal there are only a few fumes. If the meal is bigger, then the fumes go high. If you see lots of fumes coming up, go, because it's a very big meal. Go now! Go on! Go have fun! But come back in a few days."

"All right, I'll come back, I'll come talk to you then."

After the man who had been a buzzard worked at clearing his land for three days, the buzzard who had been a man returned. "God, it's true, I'm no good for anything," he said. "Already you've done a good job clearing the land. Look how much work you've done! My wife prefers you. Did she tell you I was good for nothing?"

"She didn't tell me much of anything. 'Why do you stink so? You reek!' is what she said."

"And what did you tell her?"

" 'Oh yes,' I said, 'I certainly do stink. It's because I'm working. In the past I used to lie to you. I never used to work. I just slept all the time. But now go see for yourself, if you want. When I burn our land, go look! Go and help me watch the fire.' "

"And will you take her along?"

"Yes," he said. And the wife went along when the burning of the trees began. He took her along. "Sit here. First, I'll clear the fire lane. I'll make a fire lane around our land," he said.

"All right," she replied. The wife sat down and prepared her husband's meal. Then they ate.

The smoke from the burning trees was coming up. It was curling up. The buzzard who had been a man thought it was his meal. He remembered. When they had exchanged clothes, the other one had said, "You'll see fumes rising in the sky."

When the smoke came up from the trees that were burning, that's when the buzzard came whooshing down. He landed right in the fire and burned up.

"Is the buzzard so stupid?" said the wife. "That's what the disgusting thing deserved, dying like that."

"It was the command of Our Lord," said the husband. "But never mind. Our corn will be harvested now. In a week we'll come to plant it."

"All right!" said the wife. They left. They went home. "See here," said the husband, "I'm just covered with soot. I'll change. It's because I sweat so. That's why you say I stink."

How would she know he was a buzzard?

Do you know how it was discovered? A neighbor said to her, "Oh, why don't you want to admit it? Your husband turned into a buzzard."

She told her husband, "I was right that you stink so! You see, you're a buzzard."

"Oh, what concern is that of ours?" he said. "What people won't come and tell you! Who knows if it's so?"

"Ha, how come it isn't true? I was right, it's a buzzard's stink. I was right that you're a buzzard."

"Who knows?" he said. "I never felt that I was a buzzard. Just because I sweat, it seems I have a bad odor."

"Oh, forget it," she said, "so long as you provide for me."

They had things now. They ate now. The woman's husband wasn't a loafer anymore. He worked well.

Those are the ancient words.

Tzotzil

Tup and the Ants

There was once an old man who had three sons. When they had grown up, and he had said to them, "Now you must marry," the eldest wrapped some food, asked for his father's blessing, and set out to find a wife. Meeting a man who had three daughters, he promptly married the eldest.

After a while the second son came along and married the second daughter. Finally the youngest son asked for his father's good words of blessing. Then he, too, prepared food for the road and set out to search for a bride. Before long he had joined his older brothers and in no time had married the youngest daughter of the old man.

Now Tup, the youngest boy, was a do-nothing, as his father-in-law soon found out. He was constantly being scolded for his laziness, and his mother-in-law would say to her youngest daughter, "What use is an idle husband?"

When the time came to clear cornfields, the old man called his three sons-in-law together and told them they must start the next day. "Cut trees!" he commanded.

Next morning the brothers set out to work, carrying tortillas and corn soup to last for three days. But Tup carried only a little, because his wife's mother hated to waste corn on such a worthless son-in-law.

The two older brothers quickly found a spot that suited them and began working. But Tup went on through the forest, not stopping until he had left his brothers some distance behind. Sitting down to rest, he fell asleep. When he awoke, it was quite late in the afternoon, too late to do any work. So he gathered a few palm leaves and made himself a shelter. After he had eaten some of his tortillas and drunk some of the corn soup, he went back to sleep.

Next morning, when he awoke, all his tortillas and corn soup had disappeared. Looking around and seeing a leaf-cutter ant carrying off the last piece of tortilla, he realized that while he had slept, the ants had robbed him of his food. He picked up the ant and said, "I'll kill you un-less you take me to your nest." The ant did not refuse. When they got there, Tup knocked three times, and the lord of the nest came out. "What do you want?" he asked.

"Your people have stolen all my tortillas and corn soup," said Tup. "Either you must give me back my food or you must do my work."

The lord of the nest thought for a few moments, then said, "I will do the work." So Tup showed him where to make the cornfield and went back to his shelter to sleep while the forest was being cleared. All the ants turned out to work that night, and being so many, they had cut down all the trees and bushes by the end of three days.

On the way back to his father-in-law's, Tup passed his two brothers. But instead of clearing the forest, these two were busily making holes in the tree trunks. When the old man had said, "Cut trees," they had thought he meant cut into them instead of cut them down, and on and on they worked.

When Tup got home, the old man cried, "Here comes Idle-bones, the last to go and the first to return. Don't give him anything to eat." In spite of this, the mother-in-law managed to grind some cornmeal and make a few tortillas. Later, however, when the other two brothers arrived, the old man greeted them heartily and ordered chickens cooked.

After several days, when he judged that the fields would be dry, the old man sent his three sons-in-law to burn the brush. The older two were given large supplies of corn soup and honey, while little Tup, for being so lazy, got only a small portion of each.

The two older boys, when they got to their spot in the forest, gathered all the wood chips and twigs they could find and burned them, but the column of smoke that rose to the sky was miserably thin. Meanwhile Tup took his honey and corn soup to the ants' nest and gave it to the lord of the nest on the condition that they do the work of burning his field. Then Tup rested all day, while the ants hurried about their task, burning the entire field. The columns of smoke that rose were so thick even the sun was hidden.

But the old man thought the smoke from Tup's field came from where the other two brothers were working. So when Tup returned, he again scolded him.

When all was ready for sowing, the older brothers took three mules loaded with corn seed. Tup took only one sack. The older brothers planted a little of their corn beneath the trees, but most of it they left in a storage hut

they had built in the forest, and the rest they hid in one of the hollowed-out tree trunks.

Tup, meanwhile, took his seed to the ants, but when they saw such a small sack they said it was not enough. The fire had spread far beyond the cleared area, they said, and the amount of land to be planted was now enormous. "You may find more seed in my brothers' storehouse," said Tup, and when they had started to work, he went to sleep. After the planting was done, the three returned home. Tup received his usual contemptuous welcome, while the older brothers were feasted.

When the corn was in ear, the old man sent the three sons-in-law back to their fields to make earth ovens and roast the young corn. The two older brothers, with little else they could do, dug a small hole in the ground, then put in the few stunted ears that had just managed to survive in the shade of the forest. As for Tup, he went straight to the lord of the ants, and all the ants came immediately to his aid. They brought fifteen loads of the yellow ears, made the earth oven, heated it, and packed it with the corn while Tup slept. Toward evening he awoke and returned home.

On the following day the old man and his wife, his three daughters, and their husbands set out with a team of mules to harvest the fields and eat the roasted ears. Arriving at the cornfield of the two older brothers, the father-in-law found that there was no clearing to be seen and no corn except for the few miserable plants growing in the shade of the forest, and these were more like grass than corn. When the old man saw the heap of rotting corn in the hollowed-out tree, he cried, "Where is your earth oven?"

The tiny oven was uncovered, and when the father-in-law had been shown the handful of stunted ears, he flew into a rage. Refusing even to speak to the two older brothers, he turned to Tup and said, "Let us see if you have done any better."

They started off again, Tup leading them through the forest until they came to the path the ants had made from the ant nest to the field. The path gradually widened, becoming a highway. "Where does this fine road lead?" asked the old man, and Tup replied, "To my cornfield."

Eventually they reached a huge field, stretching farther than the eye could see. "This," said Tup, "is my field." But the old man, knowing his son-in-law, could not believe it. As they climbed a small hill at the edge of the clearing, the old man's wife asked Tup where the earth oven was, thinking he would not be able to answer her, for she, too, doubted that this could be his cornfield. "You are standing on it," replied Tup. "This hill is the earth oven." Then the old man said, "You have worked enough. Let your two brothers uncover the roasted ears."

While the brothers worked, the mother-in-law tried to walk the field to see how wide and how long it might be, but it was so immense she got lost, and Tup, once again, had to call his friends the ants. Told that the old woman had lost her way, the ants spread out over the cornfield, searching until they found her.

After they had all eaten their fill of the roasted young ears and the mules had been loaded, they started for home. That night chickens were killed in honor of Tup. As for the other two brothers, they were ordered out of the house and told never to return.

Yucatec

The Corn in the Rock

I will tell you another. I have heard what the ancestors used to say, and this is what they told me.

The animals were hungry, it seems, and could get no food, the peccary, the wood pig, the paca, and all their friends. They looked for food, but they found nothing.

Except, when they met the fox they saw that his stomach was full, and they noticed his smelly belching. "Now, what did you get that your belly's so full and you smell so bad?" they wanted to know.

He refused to tell them.

But the animals talked privately among themselves and

decided to watch him. "Where does he go?" they said. They followed him and saw him go into a hole in the rock. Then they knew they had found his den.

They said to the flea, "Go after him and see what he eats," and after a long walk the flea found the fox and crept into his fur. But by this time he was tired, and he fell asleep. The next day, when the fox passed by, the flea dropped off, and all he could say was "I can't remember."

"What about you, tick?" said the animals. "Maybe you're a little smarter." So the next time the fox came along they threw the tick at him, and he crept into the fox's fur. But the tick just filled his belly, and when he got back to where the other animals were, he had nothing to tell.

They talked to the firefly. "Here, take this lantern," they said, "and shine it in the fox's den." He flew off with the lantern, and when he got inside, he shined it all around and saw corn piled up. "They've found me!" cried the fox. Then the firefly came back and said, "There's corn in the rock! Hurry up!"

"But how can we get it?" they asked. "Well, let's try lightning." So they called for lightning, and three young bachelor thunderbolts came down.

The first one flashed his fire against the cliff. He put his mind and his heart to it and all his strength. But he could not split the rock, not even a finger's breadth. The second young lightning tried but could do no better. Then the third, but the same thing happened to him. The rock would not break.

Then they called to the old man lightning, and after a while he appeared. But when he understood what they wanted, he said, "How can an old man like me split the rock, sick as I am, my face swollen, my feet swollen? If those young bachelors can't split it, what can an old man do, so old and poor? But poor as I am, I will try. If I die, why, dead I shall be."

And then he said, "Come here, you, my woodpecker. Go perch against the cliff and begin to tap. Tap against the rock until you find the thinnest part, where it is hollow underneath. That is where the corn is hidden. When you hear the hollow sound, be still while I get my fire and thunder ready. When I come, don't be afraid. Just fly away head downward. Don't fly upward or I might burn you."

The woodpecker went to the cliff and did as he had been told. When he got to the hollow part of the rock, he opened his mouth and cried out, so that the old lightning would hear him. Then the old man gathered his strength and threw himself at the cliff with all his fury. As the lightning flashed, it shattered the rock. Then the corn came out like a spout of water and spilled on the ground. It rushed forth. It roared like a river.

Before, all the corn had been white. But now much of it had been burned by the lightning and had turned red. Other grains were covered with smoke and had turned yellow. This was the beginning of red and yellow corn.

But the woodpecker—something happened to him. When the old man let loose his thunder, the woodpecker lost his senses. Instead of flying away head downward, as he had been told to do, he flew upward, and his head was a little burned by the lightning. That's why the woodpecker, ever since, has had a little red on the top of his head.

And here ends the story.

Rosalie

Traveling far, a young man who had started out from home to earn some money came to a hut where a giant lived with three daughters, and falling in love with the youngest, he made up his mind to stay. "You may stay and be my son-in-law," said the giant, "but only if you can perform the four tasks that I will give you." The young man agreed.

"First," said the giant, "I have a great desire to take my bath the moment I get out of bed instead of having to go all the way down to the lake. Tonight you will bring the lake up to the hut, so that when I wake in the morning I can sit on my bed and put my feet in water. Use this basket to carry it."

The young man hardly knew what to think. But the giant's youngest daughter, whose name was Rosalie, told him not to worry. That night, while everyone else was sleeping, Rosalie went down to the lake, and with her skirt she swept the water up to her father's bedside. When the giant awoke, he was astonished to find the water lapping the leg posts of his bed.

Next the giant took a large pot, threw it into the deepest river he could find, and told his future son-in-law to bring it back home. After diving many times, the young man was about to give up, for the river was so deep he could not reach the bottom. Then Rosalie told him to go with her to the riverbank that night, and she would dive. But he must call her name when she reached the bottom, otherwise she would be unable to rise to the surface again. This they did, and the following morning the giant found the pot once more in the house.

The next task was to make a cornfield of a hundred mecates. The young man must clear and burn the forest, do the planting, and at midnight of the same day bring back a load of fresh young ears. He set to work at daybreak but by sunset had accomplished practically nothing.

Then Rosalie stretched out her skirt, and all the forest was immediately felled. Using the same magic, she dried the brush, burned it, sowed the corn, raised the plants, and harvested the young ears, so that the young man was able to take them to her father at midnight.

Furious, the giant went to his wife to ask her how they could get rid of this would-be son-in-law. "We'll have him thrown from a horse," said his wife, and they arranged that she herself would turn into a mare, the giant would become the saddle and stirrups, and Rosalie would be the bridle. Rosalie, however, overheard their conversation and warned the one who loved her to treat the bridle carefully and not to spare the horse and the saddle.

Next morning the giant told the young man to go out into the savanna, where he would find a mare already saddled. He was to mount her and bring her back to the house. Meanwhile the giant and his wife and Rosalie took a short cut through the forest, and by the time the young man arrived, they had changed themselves into the fully saddled mare.

The young man, who had brought along a stout club, jumped onto the mare's back, and before she had a chance to buck, he began beating her as hard as he could. All but paralyzed by the blows, the mare was unable to throw her rider, and after a few moments she sank exhausted to the ground.

The young man returned to the hut, where a little later he was joined by the giant and his wife, bruised all over and worn out.

The son-in-law had now completed his four tasks, but the giant, going back on his word, told him there were yet more. That night Rosalie decided they must run away, while the giant and his wife would still be sore from the beating. When the two were asleep, Rosalie took a needle, a grain of white earth, and a grain of salt, and spitting on the floor, slipped quietly out of the house to meet the young man.

At daybreak the giant called to Rosalie to get up. "It's all right, Papá. I'm getting up. I'm combing my hair," replied the spittle. It spoke with the voice of the giant's daughter, so he suspected nothing.

A little later the giant again called to Rosalie, asking her if she was dressed yet. Again the spittle replied: "I'm combing my hair." By this time, however, the spittle was almost dry and could only answer in a whisper. Suspicious, the old lady went into Rosalie's room and discovered the trick that had been played on them.

Then the giant set out in pursuit of the fleeing couple,

rapidly gaining on them. When he had nearly overtaken them, Rosalie turned herself into an orange tree, and her companion disguised himself as an old man. Stopping next to the tree, the giant asked if a young couple had gone by.

"No," replied the old man, "but stay a moment and rest, and eat some of these oranges." The giant tasted the oranges and immediately lost his desire to run after his daughter and the young man. Returning to his hut, he explained to his wife that he had been unable to overtake them.

"You fool!" cried the old lady. "That orange tree was Rosalie."

Again the giant set out in pursuit. When he was once more at the point of overtaking them, Rosalie turned the horse they were riding into a church, her young man into the doorkeeper, and herself into an image of the Virgin. When the giant reached the church, he asked the doorkeeper if he had seen any sign of the missing pair.

"Hush!" replied the doorkeeper. "You must not talk here, the priest is just about to sing mass. Come inside and see our beautiful Virgin."

The giant entered the church, and the moment he laid eyes on the statue he lost all thought of pursuing the

young couple. Returning once again to his hut, he told his wife how he had seen the Virgin and had decided to come home.

"You fool, you fool!" cried the old lady. "The Virgin was Rosalie. You are too dim-witted to be of any use. I'll catch them myself."

The giant's wife set out at full speed. Rosalie and the young man traveled as fast as they could, but the old lady ran faster, and gradually she caught up with them. When she was almost within reach, Rosalie cried out, "We can't fool her, we'll have to use the needle."

Stooping down, she planted the needle in the ground, and immediately a dense thicket grew up. For the moment they were out of danger. As the old lady cut her way through the thicket, the young couple fled on. At last she got clear of the thicket and began gaining on them once more.

When her mother had nearly caught up with them, Rosalie threw down the grain of white earth, and immediately a mountain rose up. Again the couple fled away, as the old lady, half out of breath, scrambled to the top of the steep slope, then made her way down the other side.

Clear of the mountain at last, she continued on, rapidly gaining on her daughter and the young man. When she had almost overtaken them, Rosalie threw down the grain of salt, and it became an enormous sea. Rosalie herself became a sardine, the young man a shark, and their horse a crocodile. The old lady waded into the water, trying to catch the sardine, but the shark drove her off. "Very well," said the old lady. "But you must remain in the water seven years."

When the seven years were up and they were free at last, they came out on dry land and returned to the town where the young man's grandparents lived. Rosalie, however, could not enter the town, because she had not been baptized. She sent the young man ahead, telling him to return with half a bottle of holy water, and on no account was he to embrace his grandparents, for then he would instantly forget his Rosalie.

The young man arrived at his old home and greeted his grandparents, but he would not permit them to embrace him. Feeling tired, he decided to rest awhile before returning to Rosalie with the holy water. Soon he was fast asleep, whereupon his grandmother, bending over him, softly kissed him. When he awoke, therefore, he no longer had any recollection of Rosalie.

For days Rosalie waited for him to come back. At last,

one morning, seeing a little boy playing at the edge of the town, she called to him and asked him to get her some holy water. The boy brought it to her, and she bathed herself with it and entered the town. There she learned that the one she loved, at the urging of his grandparents, was about to marry another young woman.

Rosalie went straight to the grandparents' house, but the young man did not know who she was. Nevertheless, she succeeded in having the marriage postponed three days. Then she prepared a great feast and invited all the elders of the town as well as the young man she loved. In the center of the table she placed two dolls she had made: one that resembled herself; the other, the young man.

The guests arrived and sat down to the feast. Then Rosalie pulled out a whip and began thrashing the doll that represented the man.

"Don't you remember how you were told to carry water in a basket?" she cried, and "Whang!" the whip cut through the air. As it struck the doll, the man himself cried out in pain.

Again she spoke to the doll: "Don't you remember the pot at the bottom of the river and how I brought it up for you?" "Whang!" and again the young man cried out in pain.

"Don't you remember the cornfield you had to make and the fresh young ears I grew for you?"

"Whang!"

"And the seven years we spent in the sea?"

"Whang!"

Again the young man shrieked in pain. Then the memory of the past returned to him, and forgetting his bride-to-be, and with a cry of joy, he threw himself into Rosalie's arms.

Yucatec

Chac

Chac, the rain god, stole a boy and took him into the sky to be his servant. One day he said to the boy, "Go pull up yams, but be careful not to look underneath the root."

The boy went out and started to dig. After a while he began to wonder what would happen if he looked beneath the root. He pulled up a yam and looked into the hole. Far below he could see the earth. His home lay directly under him, and he could see his older brother.

Thinking he could return easily, he made a long rope, and tying one end to a tree and the other around his waist, he began to let himself down. But the rope, long as it was, did not come anywhere near the earth, and the boy found himself unable to climb back up. Then the wind blew, and he swayed back and forth. He was terrified.

When Chac noticed that his servant had not returned, he went out to look for him. Finding him hanging at the end of the rope, he hauled him up and scolded him.

Another day Chac sent the boy to get plantains, telling him to cut down only the smallest trees. But when he looked at the small trees, he said to himself, "The fruit is not big enough," and he proceeded to cut down the largest plantain tree he could find. Instead of falling in the opposite direction, the tree came toward him, increasing in size as it fell, and the boy was unable to escape. Hours later, Chac found him trapped under the fallen tree and again scolded him.

Chac had told the boy to ask the grindstone if he wanted any tortillas but under no circumstances to ask for more than one. So as soon as the boy was hungry, he called out to the grindstone, "I want many tortillas!" Enormous tortillas rained down, completely burying him. Chac pulled him out and again scolded him.

One day Chac told him to straighten up the house and clean the table and benches, because he was going to hold a feast and was expecting guests. The boy cleaned the house thoroughly, but returning later, he found many frogs seated on the benches. Annoyed that they had come in to dirty the place after he had cleaned it, he drove them out with his broom. Later Chac asked if the guests and the musicians had arrived, since it was past time for the feast.

"No, no guests have arrived yet," said the boy. "Nothing but a crowd of frogs that came into the house just after I got it all clean."

"Well," said Chac, "those were my guests and musicians."

One day the boy decided he would play at being Chac, so he watched how Chac dressed himself when he went out to do his work. At night, when Chac was asleep, the boy took his clothes, his windbag, his water gourd, his ax, and his drum. As he opened the bag, the winds went screeching off. He could not shut them up again because he was not as strong as Chac, and a terrific storm rushed down on the world.

Then he took the gourd to make rain. But unlike Chac, who could cause a heavy rain by pouring out four fingers of water, the boy spilled the whole gourd, and torrents poured down on the earth. Next he beat on the drum to make thunder, but when he tried to stop it he could not. While trying to control the thunder, the rain, and the winds, the boy fell into the sea.

When Chac woke up, his clothes and his instruments were nowhere to be seen. His servant had disappeared too. He went to one of the other Chacs and borrowed clothes and a windbag and went out to stop the rain and thunder and bag the winds. Not until he had controlled the storm did he begin looking for the boy. At last he found him, broken into many pieces. The black wind, the biggest of all the winds, had smashed him to bits. Nine times Chac made passes over the boy's body, and in this way he revived him. When they returned to Chac's house, he told the boy he could not keep him any longer, because he was always getting into trouble. Then he took him back to earth.

When the boy arrived at his home, he asked his older brother if the storm had done much damage. "Oh yes!" said the brother. Then the boy began to laugh and said, "I was the one who caused the storm. Wasn't it fun?"

Yucatec

The Lord of the Clouds

They say it happened long ago, they say a man was carried off by the lord of the clouds, who took him away to
his home in the sky, and when the man looked around,
he saw angels. They were just setting out with their capes,
just beginning to run, starting to thunder, and they made
a cracking sound. In their hands they carried a reflecting
sword that flashes when rain falls, and makes lightning.
The noise of their capes is the storm, and when they run,
rain falls on the earth.

The man saw what the angels did, and later he put on
their capes and went out by himself. Rain came, but it

was a pouring rain that never let up, a rain that made people sad and worried. When the angels heard the storm, they came to see who had caused it, and they saw the man running along. They caught him, and when they had taken him back to the house, they scolded him, and the rain let up, so it is said.

Another time, they say, the angels left the man at home to make supper, having first measured out the beans for him to cook. "Very well," he said. But after the angels had left, the man said to himself, "Ha! these beans are not enough. Better throw in a few more."

When the beans began to cook, oooh! they swelled and spread all over the floor. And to think he had said they would not be enough!

Then the angels came back and saw all the beans. "Did you throw in more beans?" they asked. "You had better go back where you came from." And the next thing the man knew, he was walking along just as he had been, before he had been carried away by the lord of the clouds.

Mam

Rabbit and Coyote

There was a man. There was a watermelon patch that this man had. And when the watermelons were getting ripe, the man went to take a look at them, and when he saw that the insides had been scraped out, he said, "Who's been eating my watermelons?"

Then he thought of a trick to catch the thief. He made a little man out of wax and put it on top of one of the watermelons.

When the thief came along—and it was Rabbit—he saw the little man sitting on the watermelon and he said, "Get off of there! If you don't get off, I'll slap you off with my hand." But when he slapped at it, his hand stuck fast in the wax.

"Let go of my hand," he said, "or I'll kick you in with my foot." But when he kicked, his foot got stuck, and he rolled off onto the ground, still trying to get loose.

When the man came back, there was Rabbit. And there was the little wax man that had tricked him. The owner of the watermelon patch picked up Rabbit and threw him into a cage and said, "Rabbit, I'm going to shame your face. Wait till I get back here with something nice and hot."

The man went home and said to his boys, "Here! Take this poker and put it in the fire. We're going to get Rabbit in the rear end."

While Rabbit was waiting, Coyote came by. "So! What's happening to you?" he says.

"Oh, shut up!" says Rabbit. "I'm just waiting for a cup of hot chocolate this man's making for me. But why don't you take my place? My stomach's so small and he's making so much, I'd never finish it. You with your big stomach could drink the whole thing."

Just then the man called out, "Sorry to keep you waiting, Rabbit. It isn't hot enough yet. But don't worry, it will be just right in a few minutes."

"You see?" said Rabbit. "He wants it to be perfect. So why don't you open this door and take my place?" Coyote unbarred the door and got inside the cage.

While Rabbit was running away, the man sent his boys to the watermelon patch with the hot poker. "Ya! This rabbit's a big one!" they said when they got to the cage. Then they gave it to him in the rear end, and Coyote felt the fire.

"Now I've had it!" said Coyote, and he ran off looking for Rabbit. Pretty soon he found him, settled down at the edge of a sapodilla grove.

"Ya! What are you doing just sitting there?" says Coyote. "I'm ready to finish you off right now!"

"Oh, shut up," says Rabbit. "Come on, let's eat these sapodillas. Look, here's a ripe one all for you, just about to fall into your mouth. Open up wide."

"All right," said Coyote. He opened his mouth as wide as he could, and Rabbit threw in a green sapodilla and broke all his teeth.

Rabbit ran off fast. When Coyote found him again, he was drinking at a well. "Now I've got you," he says.

"Oh, shut up, Uncle Coyote! Burnt Bottom! Gums!" says Rabbit. "Look, there's a cheese down in this well. But it's so deep, I can't drink up enough water to get to

it. My stomach's too small. But you with your big stomach could hold it all."

"All right," said Coyote, and he started to drink. He drank, but the well never went dry. He drank until his stomach exploded.

And where was the cheese? What was it but the moon's reflection shining in the water? Well, that was the end of poor Coyote.

Mam-Kekchi

Rabbit and Puma

Big Puma was always looking for Rabbit, and one day he found him under an overhanging rock. Rabbit had no time to escape, but as soon as he saw Puma coming, he reached up with his front paws and began to push against the rock.

"I've got you now," said Puma.

"But you can't eat me."

"I'm going to."

"Don't even think it!" said Rabbit. "I'm holding up the roof of the world. If I let go now, the sky will fall."

"Is this true?" said Puma. Puma began debating with himself what to do.

"I'm straining as hard as I can," said Rabbit. "You had better help me. If I have to let go, we'll both be killed."

"Then I had better help you."

"Now, hold it firm," said Rabbit. "I'm going to go look for a couple of sticks to prop it up. If you see that I don't come soon, pull that little bell beside you, and when I hear it, I'll come running."

Big Puma braced himself against the rock, while Rabbit eased to one side and scampered away.

Puma began to feel tired. He pulled the bell. But what he had been told was a bell was not a bell. It was a wasps' nest. The wasps began to sting him, and he came running out from under the rock. When he saw that the sky did not fall, he said to himself, "Rabbit has fooled me too much."

After a while he met Rabbit again, hanging on to the end of a vine, going up and down, up and down.

"Devil vine, shrink!" Rabbit would say, and the vine would shorten up, pulling him to the top of the tree. "Devil vine, stretch!" he would say, and it would lengthen out and carry him back to the ground. He pretended not to notice Puma and went on with his game.

"You won't fool me again," said Puma. "As soon as I catch hold of that vine, you're going to be eaten."

"Oh no, you have the wrong rabbit!" he cried. But Puma would not change his mind. The moment the end of the vine touched the ground, he grabbed it and started to yank. But Rabbit quickly jumped off and gave the order "Shrink!"

All at once poor Puma was jerked to the top of the tree. Rabbit ran and hid.

When Puma tried to come down to earth again, he could not remember the word to make the vine stretch. He thought and thought, but it was no use. Finally he had to let himself drop, and he fell to earth and was bruised all over.

The next time Puma met Rabbit, he found him picking up hay in a hay patch. "Rabbit," he said, "now I must eat you. You have fooled me too much."

"Wait," said Rabbit, "I've got a good offer for this hay in the village. Why don't you help me? We'll split the profits. I'm small and can't carry much, but you have a big strong back and could carry two loads."

Big Puma agreed, and they piled the two loads on his back and tied them with a rope. They had not walked far when Rabbit said, "Oh, how tired I am already!" and he climbed on top of the two loads and began to ride along. Then he lit a match and pushed it into the hay.

As soon as Rabbit saw that the hay was burning, he jumped off and ran away. The dry hay flared like a torch, and big Puma was burned up for good.

After that, Rabbit lived in peace.

Yucatec-Tzutuhil

Rabbit Gets Married

A story of the ancestors, long ago. A story of Rabbit and Coyote's daughter. It was in those days that the two met, this Coyote woman, this Rabbit man. It was then that Rabbit said, "Let's get married."

"It wouldn't do," she said. "You're too short for me."

"Not as short as you think," said Rabbit. And with that he took hold of her. She was annoyed. "Do it again and I'll catch you in my mouth and eat you." He did it again.

She was just about to catch him when Rabbit ran off. He squeezed through a log fence, and Coyote's daughter dashed after him so fast the logs tumbled down and made a trap, and she couldn't get free.

Then Rabbit teased her. He started to caress her. "So you think I'm short."

"Oh no, you're tall," she said. "You're very tall."

Just then Coyote himself came along. Rabbit looked up and saw him. "Hurry," he said. "Hurry up! Look what your daughter did. She's in jail."

"Why?" said the father.

"Because of a crime she committed. She tried to steal somebody and ended up in jail."

"Help me get her free," said Coyote. "Help me!" So Rabbit helped, but he was too small. He wasn't strong enough to lift the logs.

"If we don't get my daughter free, I'll eat you," said Coyote. "I'll eat you so fast you'll come out my rear end with the fur still on. Pull with me now. We'll do it together."

"But don't you see how small I am?" said Rabbit. "I'm not strong enough."

"We'll both pull at once," said Coyote. "Now what?"

Rabbit was thinking. He thought he would call for help. And who did he call? A puma who was just passing by.

Puma came over, and Puma and Coyote both pulled at once—while Rabbit sat back and took it easy. Pretty soon Puma bit one of the logs with his teeth. The log flipped over on top of them both, setting Coyote's daughter free. She immediately ran off with Rabbit.

"I think my father's been killed," she said. "Oh! I'm afraid he's been killed."

"No, no," said Rabbit. "Don't worry. Let's go! Let's go away and be married forever." And that's what they did.

Kanhobal

Lord Sun's Bride

In a house deep in the woods an old man was living with his only daughter, a pretty young woman who could spin cotton quickly and weave to perfection. Spying on her, the sun decided to make her his wife and thought he would win her on his own, without the help of a match-maker.

The next day he went hunting, shot a deer, and carried it past the young woman's house. Game was scarce, but Lord Sun had a plan to trick the girl into thinking he was a hunter who always came back with plenty.

Having stuffed the deerskin with ashes and grass and

dried leaves, he would take it into the woods every evening after dark and leave it there. Then he would go back
to his hut. Early in the morning he would pass by the
girl's house empty-handed, returning a little later with
the stuffed animal on his shoulder.

"Look, Father," said the old man's daughter, "that
hunter shoots game every day. I think he should be my
husband."

"Ah," said the old man, "he may be tricking you."

"Oh no," she replied, "he has to be the one who kills
the game. Look at the blood on him."

"Well," said the father, "throw some water on the path
when he comes by again, and see what happens."

The girl didn't believe him. But the next time she saw
Lord Sun on his way home from hunting, she took some
of the lime water she had been using to soak corn and
threw it on the path.

Lord Sun slipped and fell. The deerskin burst, and all
the ashes and grass and leaves poured out on the ground.
The young woman began to laugh, and Lord Sun ran off.

He was ashamed. Then he went to the hummingbird
and asked to borrow the bird's skin. The hummingbird
at first refused, saying he would die of the cold, agree-
ing only after Lord Sun had promised to wrap him in

cotton. When the exchange had been made, Lord Sun put on the skin, turned into a hummingbird, and flew back to the young woman's house.

From the ashes and leaves that had poured out of the deer hide, a tobacco plant had sprung up, and it was already in flower. Sun flew directly to it and began sucking the nectar, darting from blossom to blossom. When the young woman saw him, she called to her father.

"Look, Father, a hummingbird! Get your blowgun and shoot him. I want him for a pet."

"Very well," said the old man, and he aimed the blowgun so that the bird was only stunned. "Look for it in the grass," he said. When she found it, it was softly chirping: sweet sweet swee. As she stooped down to pick it up, the strap that passed around her waist to hold the loom tight slipped, and the loom fell to the ground.

She carried the hummingbird indoors and, giving it chocolate and corn syrup, succeeded in reviving it. Then she took it to her bedroom, which was the innermost of thirteen rooms, and as the darkness was now coming fast, she laid the bird aside and went to sleep.

In the middle of the night she awoke and found a man lying next to her. It was Lord Sun. "My father will kill me," she said.

"Not if we run away," he replied.

The girl wanted to go with him very much, but she was afraid. Her father, they say, had a magic stone in which he could see everything that was happening in the world. "Give me the stone," said Lord Sun, and when she had brought it to him, he smeared it with soot and told her to put it back in its place. Now, he thought, they could leave without danger of being seen.

But the girl was still afraid, because her father had a magic blowgun with which he could suck anything to him, no matter how far away it might be. "Where is the blowgun?" asked Lord Sun.

"Here," she replied. Then he told her to grind some dried chilis. When the chili pepper was ready, he poured it into the blowgun and told the girl to put it back in its place. As soon as she had done so, they slipped away.

Next morning when the old man awoke, he saw no sign of his daughter and heard no sound in the house. He called to her and got no reply. He looked for her and failed to find her. Then he reached for his magic stone to discover where she might have gone. But he could see nothing because the stone was blackened with soot. At last, however, he found a small spot that Lord Sun had neglected to cover up, and looking closely, he saw his daughter and a young man out on the water in a canoe.

Reaching quickly for his magic blowgun, he put it to his lips and sucked in as hard as he could. The next moment he lay on his back, gasping for air and coughing violently: ochó, ochó, ochó. And that was the first coughing in the world.

The old man was furious. "Now they shall die," he said. Then he called to the rain god, Chac, and when Chac arrived, he ordered him to send a thunderbolt to kill the fleeing couple.

Chac protested. "No, I won't kill them. You hate them now and want them dead. But later, when your anger passes, you will be sorry, and you will be angry with me for having killed them."

But the old man insisted. Finally Chac threw on his black clothes, took up his drum and his ax, and departed. Traveling high in the sky, he looked down and caught sight of the canoe.

Sun saw him coming. "Your father has sent Chac to kill us," he cried. "Quick, jump into the water!" Immediately he changed himself into a turtle, and the young woman became a crab, both of them swimming downward as fast as they could.

Lord Sun was far below the surface in no time. But the

crab swims slowly, and when the lightning struck, the girl was only a little way down. She was killed instantly, and her blood flowed in all directions.

When the danger had passed, Lord Sun rose to the surface again and saw the young woman's blood in the water. Grief-stricken, he called to the small fish that lived there and asked them to help him. But instead, they began drinking the blood. Then he called to the dragonfly. It answered him: srrr srrr srrr. He ordered it to collect all the blood, and it obeyed him at once, filling thirteen water jars. These Lord Sun left in the house of an old woman who lived by the shore, promising to return in thirteen days.

When the thirteen days had passed, he came back and asked for the jars. "Take them away," cried the old woman. "I can't sleep for the noise that comes from inside them, a buzzing and a humming and a rustling."

Lord Sun began to pour out the jars. The first contained nothing but snakes, all kinds of poisonous snakes. The second and third jars were also full of snakes, though not poisonous. The fourth was full of mosquitoes. In the fifth were sand flies; in the sixth, green hornets; in the seventh, yellow wasps; in the eighth, small black wasps; in the ninth, black wasps with white wings; in the tenth, stinging caterpillars; and in the eleventh and twelfth, all sorts of flies. Before this time, these creatures had not been known in the world.

But in the thirteenth jar he found his love, alive again and as beautiful as she had been before. Then he called to a deer and ordered it to carry her into the sky. It did so, and there she remained, becoming our heavenly mother, the moon.

Kekchi

The Lost Children

One day a woman told her husband to go lose their children because there was not enough food to feed them, and the next day the man took the children into the woods and left them there. The boy had been eating a lime and had dropped the peelings as they went along. So he and his sister were able to find their way back to the house. When they got there, they sat down outside the door and began to cry.

The woman scolded her husband for not doing a better job of losing the children, and the next day he took them much farther. This time they were unable to return, for now they were deep in the hill country. But God gave them two dogs to guide them.

Continuing on, they met a giant, who offered to take them to his house. In the course of time the sister became the giant's wife. Disgusted, the brother went off, taking the dogs with him. The giant, who had wanted to kill the boy from the day he had first seen him, set out in pursuit and soon caught up. Seeing the giant, the boy climbed into a tree, and from there he called out to his dogs. Being intelligent, the dogs understood what their master was saying to them, and they jumped on the giant and killed him.

As soon as the sister found out what had happened, she went and picked up one of the giant's bones, sharpened it, and hid it under her brother's pillow. When he lay down to sleep, it punctured him through the ear, and he died. He was carried off to be buried, with the dogs following behind. The dogs stayed in the cemetery, and at night they dug him up and kept licking his ear until he came back to life. Then they gave him much good advice, and when at last he had told them good-bye, they spread out their wings, like angels, and flew up to heaven.

Kekchi

The Bad Compadre

A merchant named Mariano went to sell a little bread and a little sugar and a little meat. He went to make a journey, and when he returned, he brought much money.

His compadre, Juan, heard about it. Then Juan said to his wife, "Do me a favor, do me an errand. Go see our compadre, maybe talk to his wife." The woman went, she talked to the man. "Do me a favor, compadre. Sometime when you go on a trip, tell your compadre. Do him that favor. 'I'll follow along, I want to make that trip' is what your compadre is saying."

"All right," said Mariano, "I'll be gone for a week, and

I'll earn a little money. I'll buy a little bread and a little meat and a little sugar and a little sausage. That's what I'll take with me."

"Thank you, I'll tell your compadre," and she returned to her husband and told him what Mariano had said.

"Well, all right," said Juan. "I'll be gone for a week, but I won't take much with me, only a little bread and a little meat and a little sugar and a little sausage. That's what I'll take, I'll take it and sell it." So Juan got a little money and bought the bread and bought the meat and bought the sugar and bought the sausage. A week later he went on the business trip with his compadre. They went together.

Now Mariano knew magic, and when Juan lagged behind, Mariano went on ahead and made a spell. A swarm of leaf-cutter ants appeared, and he left them there in the road. When Juan came along, he could not get by them. Quickly he put down his bag and took out four pounds of sugar, pouring it in front of the leaf-cutter ants, together with half the bread. And with that they went running off the road.

When Juan caught up with his compadre, he found him in the shade.

"Well," said Mariano, "why don't you walk faster? I've been here a long time. I've been waiting for you."

"Well, yes, compadre," replied Juan. "I walk slowly." And again his compadre set off at full speed and Juan lagged behind.

Juan came to a bend in the road, and right there in front of him were two snakes. Frightened, he quickly took out two pounds of meat, one pound for one snake, one pound for the other. After eating the meat, they gave him permission to pass.

When at last he caught up, his compadre said, "Well, why can't you walk faster?" and "What have you been doing?"

"Nothing, compadre."

"Come on, let's go. Time is passing."

"All right," said Juan.

Then Mariano went off at full speed, and Juan lagged behind again. He was not a good traveler. When he got to a turn in the road, he saw two coyotes. Quickly he took out all the bread that was left and half the meat. He gave it to them, and they ate it up. Then they ran off into the woods, and Juan went on and caught up with his compadre.

"Well, compadre, what happened to you?"

"Nothing, compadre."

"Why were you so far behind?"

"Well, compadre, I got a little tired."

"Come on, let's go. Already the sun is going down."

"All right, compadre," said Juan. Then Mariano ran on ahead and made more magic. He made two hawks appear and left them there in the road. Poor Juan was unable to pass, because the hawks were ready to eat him. Quickly he took out all the sausage and threw it in front of them. They carried it right off, giving him permission to pass. Continuing on, he caught up with his compadre.

"Well, compadre," said Mariano, "can't you go a little faster?"

"Well, yes, compadre, but I got a little tired. I had to slow down."

"Compadre, I'm going to tell you something. Don't fall behind anymore, because we're just about to reach the plantation that I'm headed for."

"All right," said Juan. Then Mariano ran ahead and made more magic against his compadre. He called up two jaguars, and when Juan came along, there they were, right in the middle of the road, waiting to eat him. Juan was frightened. But he took out his last piece of meat and threw it in front of the jaguars, and they ran off. That was all the meat he had, and Mariano had hoped he would be killed. But God did not give the jaguars permission to eat poor Juan.

When he caught up with his compadre, Mariano said, "Oh, why can't you walk faster?"

"Well, yes, compadre, I do walk slowly."

"Did you meet any animals on the road?"

"No, I didn't see any."

"Well, don't lag so far behind, because we're almost to the plantation."

"All right, compadre."

By the time they arrived at the plantation, the sun had gone down, and they had to look for a place to sleep. But first Mariano went to the owner of the plantation and talked to him. "I've brought along a servant who works wonderfully. And you will see for yourself how he does everything I say. And well, tomorrow I will show you this servant. But such a servant! He works wonderfully! Wonderfully!"

"All right, all right," said the owner. "Let's leave it at that."

Next morning Mariano brought his compadre to work, and when evening came, the poor man returned very tired. Then the bad Mariano went to the owner again and said, "Now, patrón, I am going to tell you something. You give me a little money because I found our servant. And let me tell you what this servant told me. He said, 'I don't want this work, it's too easy.' That's what he told me. And then he said, 'I'll mix a quintal of sugar and a quintal of salt, the two quintals mixed, and when morning comes I'll give you the sugar in one bag and the salt in another.' This is how our servant talks, patrón!"

"Well, all right," said the owner, "and if he doesn't do it, I'll have him punished."

Then the owner called poor Juan. "Look here, son, is it true that you say you can sort out a quintal of sugar and a quintal of salt from two quintals mixed?"

"Señor, I do not say anything," replied Juan.

"Oh yes you do," said Mariano. "My servant speaks only the truth."

"Well now, we'll give you a quintal of each," said the owner. And at that very moment, right in front of poor Juan, they mixed the salt with all the sugar. Now it was done.

At eight o'clock that night Juan went to sleep, and the poor man quickly dreamed. He dreamed that the ants were saying to him, "Son, do not worry. We will take care of it, and at six in the morning you will find a bag of sugar and a bag of salt. Yes, it is true, and the bags will be well filled."

Morning came. Mariano said, "Did you do what we talked about?"

"Compadre, I did not do anything."

Mariano went to look at the bags, and there they were, the salt and the sugar, completely separated. He went running to the owner of the plantation. "Patrón, patrón," he called at the door.

The patrón got out of bed. "What do you want?"

"Señor, come quickly. Our servant has done it. What I told you was not a lie. Our servant works wonderfully. And let me tell you what he told me. He says he wants to do something big. So I said to him, 'Make a cornfield of five hundred mecates. Make it on the side of the mountain and have it ready by six tomorrow morning.' And he says, 'So what? I can do it.' That's what he said, patrón."

"All right," said the patrón, "I will call the man."

"Now, is it true that you say you can have a cornfield of five hundred mecates ready by six o'clock tomorrow morning?"

"Señor, I say nothing."

"Oh no," said Mariano. "Our servant tells the truth. Five hundred mecates by tomorrow morning. Have your foreman there at half past five."

Juan was silent.

That night the animals came. They cleared the forest and planted the cornfield. At three o'clock the foreman was sent for. He went with the other men. They went to see the cornfield, and it was true. There it was. The foreman measured it. Five hundred mecates, all done. Then he came back and delivered the record of it to the owner of the plantation.

Then the bad compadre went by another road to see the patrón. He said to him, "You see, I told you how well our servant works. But now, patrón, he says, 'I wish they would tell me to make a four-story house with a clock at the top, and the clock with four bells in it, and the house all plastered and whitewashed inside, with a garden and a water tank in front, and the lady of the house, the daughter of the patrón, with a beautiful new baby at her breast, by five o'clock tomorrow morning. All these things I would do.' That's what our servant says, patrón, and our servant speaks only the truth."

"Well, thanks to my servant if he will do me that favor," said the patrón. "And let us see if he can bring a child to the breast of my daughter! If he does not, I will turn him over for punishment. And all the work must be finished tomorrow morning at six. Now let me call him. Juan, come here!"

"Señor," answered Juan.

"Can you really do what you say, my servant? Is it true you can do all this work?"

"Señor, I say nothing."

"And it must be done by six tomorrow morning."

"As you wish, señor," said Juan. And Juan went to sleep. He dreamed. He did not dream thoughts. Rather, all the animals spoke to him in his sleep.

"Juan, we are telling you not to worry. We will do the work," said the animals in his dream. And it was true. They did the work in one night. The coyotes made the bricks. The snakes did the plastering. The hawks laid the bricks, and the leaf-cutter ants brought the beams.

The hawks went to get the clock. They both went. One brought the clock, and one brought the child from another country. All these things they brought, and they finished the whole house and painted it. And when the daughter of the patrón went inside, she felt nothing. But once inside, she felt a child at her breast.

When morning came, there was the garden, and there

was the water tank, all well made. At six o'clock the owner of the plantation arrived. He looked, and there was the garden and all the rest, done in one night.

Then Mariano went to the owner and said, "Patrón, now you see what I told you. The servant is very good, this servant of ours. All he promised, all of it he has done. And you will pay me well, because I am the one who told you he would do it."

"All right, Mariano, I will pay you well, because now I have a big house with a clock. Yes, I will pay you well. Come get your money this afternoon."

"All right, patrón. But Juan will be coming to ask you for money too. Don't give him much. No, give it to me, because I found the man."

"All right," said the patrón.

That afternoon at five o'clock, Mariano and his compadre both went to get their pay. The patrón gave poor Juan only a little, while Mariano got much.

That night Juan slept at the plantation, as he had done before. And in his dream the animals said to him, "Poor Juan, it is a shame what Mariano has done to you, what has happened to you because of your compadre, how he has mistreated you, and all because we did you a favor and did the work for you ourselves. Now the place has been pointed out where we will be waiting for Mariano. Do not be afraid. We will catch hold of him, and we will take his life, because we feel badly about what happened, and it is better that his bones remain in that place.

"You are free, because the sin is Mariano's. You bought the meat, you made the expense, and now, in that place, we will put in your hand all the money he has. When we take the money, we will give it to you, Juan." This is what they told him in his dream.

In the morning he arose, and it was true. When he arrived at that place, there were the animals in the road with his compadre, Mariano, who had gone on ahead. The animals caught hold of him, but they did nothing to Juan. The punishment of God was on his compadre, and all his bones remained in that place.

Then when Juan reached his town, Mariano's wife went to see him.

"Hello, compadre."

"Come in, comadre."

"Please, compadre, in what place did your compadre stay?"

Juan said to her, "Comadre, he took too many drinks, and because he feels a little sick, he will be delayed. He stays in the tavern."

"All right, compadre. Well, thank you. Then he will come in a little while."

Cakchiquel

Blue Sun

I will tell you another, I know another, told by the ancestors long ago.

There was an old woman who had two grandchildren. The older boy was named Blue Sun. His brother was called Youngest of the Family. Every day these two went off to work, went walking off. And every day Blue Sun would kill his little brother. When he returned home alone, the grandmother would ask, "Where did your younger brother stay?"

"I don't know," the boy would tell her. "He stayed to play somewhere. I didn't see where he stayed."

Sometimes it would be already dark when the younger boy came home. At other times he would arrive just a little later than his brother. This happened because the older boy would kill him, cut off his head, and throw it away. Yet he never died. He would gather himself together again and come back to life. And again his brother would kill him, take off his head, and throw it into a hole. Then he would cut up his body. But bees and wasps would always come to collect the pieces and say the words to make them stick together again.

One day, after he had returned home, the younger boy noticed his grandmother making thread out of cotton, the cottonseed piled up at her side. The boy came over to her, picked up a handful of seed, and went out to the woods. As he threw the cottonseed into an old tree, it turned into a beehive, and that was the beginning of honey. Then the boy went and found his older brother and said, "Come on, there's honey. Let's go eat some."

"You're joking, your eyes deceive you."

"No, the honey is right there," said the younger brother.

"Let's go, then. But if there's none, you know what will happen. You won't come back alive."

"But it's really there. Come on."

When they reached the foot of the tree, the older boy saw the honey and climbed up. While his brother remained on the ground, he scooped out the honey and began eating it right there in the top of the tree.

"Give me some, too," said his younger brother.

"Wait!" he said, and he went on eating. Then he picked out the beeswax and called, "Where are you, boy?"

"Here I am."

"Stand out in the open." Then the younger boy stood away from the tree while his brother aimed a perfect shot and hit him in the head.

"Ouch," he cried, "I'm done for!" But he picked up the wax, held it tightly, and stuck a piece of sharpened palm wood into the top end. When it was finished, he laid it at the foot of the tree.

He asked for another. "Give me some more," he said, and again he was hit on the head. He picked up the wax, squeezed it, gave it teeth, just as he had done before, and set it near the tree beside the first one.

Now, it seems he had a machete, a very small machete, and he was beginning to cut at the base of the tree. His older brother heard the cutting noise and shouted, "What are you doing? Don't cut the tree down with me in it."

"What would I cut you down with? This little machete?" And he showed him how small it was. Then he asked for more wax, and it was tossed down. With the wax he made one more image and placed it at the foot of the tree. Immediately it set to work, they say, for these were the first gophers. Their teeth were the palm-wood sticks that the younger brother had given them, and the reason gophers have no bones, so the ancestors used to say, is that they were made from beeswax.

The gophers worked, cutting through the roots, and when the tree toppled over, it killed the older brother. He was smashed to bits. The larger pieces of his body became the larger animals, the deer, the paca, and the wood pig, and all sorts of other creatures. The smaller pieces became the birds that fly in the sky. And in this way all the animals in the world came into being, so said the ancestors, and it was told to me, too. So I am telling you what the ancestors said long ago.

My grandfather also told me that when the younger brother arrived home, according to the ancestors, his grandmother asked, "Where is your older brother? You're never the one who comes home first."

"I don't know," he replied. "He stayed somewhere. I didn't see where he stayed."

"You probably killed him."

"No, why would I kill him?"

The old woman waited. He didn't appear. She was sad, she was asking questions.

"Don't be sad," said her grandchild. "Animals just for you will be coming soon. Shell some corn, for they will surely come. When they do, you must feed them right away. Then you must choose the ones you like. Catch them and hold them, and they will be your pets."

So the old woman shelled corn and put it into a basket. When the animals came, she fed it to them. Then she caught hold of the ones she liked, holding them all together in one hand.

"Don't laugh at them," her grandchild warned her. "If you laugh at them, all gathered in your hand, their tails will come off. You'll have nothing left but the tails. The rest of them will escape."

But the animals were jumping around as she held their tails, and she started to laugh. Yes, the old woman laughed. Off came the tails of all the animals she had caught, the deer, the wood pig, the rabbit, and the paca, all those that have no tails today. They were afraid of being laughed at, so they started to run away, and that's when their tails came off.

The ancestors say that the only thing she caught afterward was the rabbit, which she is still holding today. They say that she is our heavenly mother, the moon, and her rabbit can be seen in her arms.

And as many animals as ate the corn are still eating corn today, the paca, the wood pig, and others, also the birds that eat corn, the crow, the grackle, and others. Yet other birds do not eat corn now, because they did not get corn to eat then. That's what the ancestors said long ago.

I, too, can tell it, because it was told to me. What I tell you is what the ancestors said. Whatever they told they believed, they respected whatever it was.

Tzeltal

The Charcoal Cruncher

There was a man, and he had a wife. The man touched his wife in the dark. But she wasn't there, just her body was there. She had no head. He lit his lantern. That man was scared. The next night it happened again.

She would get up every night. "Why do you do this?" he asked. "Where are you going?" Her awful head wouldn't answer. The man would just hear her gnawing charcoal at the fireside, gnawing at night like a rat. She grabbed those coals and crunched away on them, the ones that were burning—not the extinguished ones—the hot ones.

Or else you could hear her bumping around behind the house if there wasn't any charcoal at the fireside. Wherever she went to crunch charcoal, she would bump, scaring people outside the house, next to the house—wherever she went.

At dusk and at dawn, at dusk and at dawn, the man was sick and tired of it. The woman was hardly good company, not even when he sat down to chat with her. She would keep nodding off. All she did was nod her head. You never saw good talk or laughter. She only nodded off.

Or if they went to bed, she would leave and go from yard to yard, bumping around, or arriving with a sudden thud at a neighbor's fireside.

The man told his mother, "I don't know what to do. I'm just sick and tired of her. I'm dying of fright, Mother. I'm scared to death, Mother. In the night you touch the awful woman, just the ugly stump of her neck, nothing to talk to. You think you'll rest her head on your arm. Where would you find it? Who knows where her head is?"

"Spy on her, son!" said his mother.

The man spied on his wife to see when she went out to eat charcoal, to see if she was thudding around outside. When she had had her child, she hadn't gone out as often. But now that the baby was big and didn't nurse anymore, the husband would be left hugging his child while the woman went bumping around to the neighbors' houses.

When he saw that his wife wasn't there, he did as his mother had told him to do. He stuck his fingers in the saltcellar and carefully rubbed the salt on his wife's neck. When she came back, she began bouncing around on the bed. Her head was just flopping about like a chicken. She landed on top of her little child. "Ow!" cried the baby.

The woman kept banging about. Her head wouldn't stick on. "Why is it?" she said. "Where can I go, now that my body doesn't fasten on anymore?"

"I don't know. See for yourself!" said her husband. "I don't want to be with you any longer."

Her head bounced. It landed on his shoulder. The man now had two heads, a man's head and a woman's head. "This is terrible," he said. "I have two faces, one a woman's, the other a man's."

Maybe it was a week or ten days that the awful woman's head was stuck there. The man said to his mother, "My shoulder's worn out. 'Get off, my shoulder's tired!'

I try to tell her. But she won't pay any attention. I think I'll go for a walk, Mother. I think I'll see if there's a place I can lure her to and leave her, if there's some kind of berry for her to eat in the woods.''

They went looking for fruit. It was pine nuts. That was it. ''Stay here, wife, I'll go get some fruit for us to eat,'' he told her.

''All right,'' she said, and her head came off and sat on the ground.

The man climbed to the top of the pine. ''Well, woman, do you think I'm coming down?'' he said. ''Go die somewhere!''

Oh, she tried to bounce up, but she couldn't reach him. She only had the strength to reach halfway up the pine tree. She came crashing down. Just then a deer was passing by. She landed sitting on its shoulder. Stuck onto it, she went off, indeed!

The deer simply sprinted off, since it had a burden now, you see. The deer left, carrying it away. You see, that's how the Charcoal Cruncher disappeared long ago. To this day there aren't any. We never hear of Charcoal Crunchers now. The end.

Tzotzil

How a Witch Escaped

Once, long ago, there was a trembling in the earth, and people said an old witch was bothering the great horned snake who lived underground. With every ache she gave him he moved and shook the earth, they told each other. So they went to their chief and said, "Have this witch burned in the marketplace."

The chief's messengers went to the witch's cave. When they got there, she said, "Yes, dear people, I will go with you, but first I must tell my boatmen good-bye." She went over to the picture of a boat she had outlined with ashes on the floor of the cave, stepped into it, and was rowed away. The messengers heard the splash of oars in the water. Then all was quiet.

The chief was angry when the messengers told him how the old woman had disappeared. But since the earth had stopped trembling, he calmed down and said, "Perhaps she will drown on her voyage and be killed by water instead of by fire."

Before long, however, the earth began shaking again, and it shook so hard that birds, beasts, and snakes left their homes in the mountains and came into the towns. Rivers left their beds and overflowed the fields, and the horned snake under the ground belched up fire and ashes through a hole in the side of a mountain.

Again the people went to their chief. "We have prayed to the Lord of the Thirteen Hills," they cried, "but he is powerless to save our cornfields unless you burn the witch."

Once again the chief sent his messengers to the witch's cave. Again she said, "Yes, dear people, I will go with you." But she added, "First let me find my ball of maguey thread." When she had found it, she went with them peaceably to the market square, where a crowd had gathered to see her burned alive.

She heard the charges against her, then said, "It is true,

O chief, that I can calm the horned serpent, whose restlessness is caused by a worm in his tooth. But first I must go to the clouds for a medicine to be found only there, for that alone will kill the worm."

"Go quickly," said the chief. Then she drove a three-pronged stick into the ground, tied the loose end of the maguey thread to it, threw the ball into the air, climbed up the slender rope, and was never seen again.

Kekchi

The Mole Catcher

It was in the ancient days, and Nuxi was catching moles. He caught many moles, then lost his way, and already the sun was beginning to set. It was very low. Nuxi, the ancient one, spoke to himself. "I am lost," he said.

Then he climbed up into a golden spoon tree and was eating the fruit, when he saw someone approaching on the ground below. "A woman!" he said. "And she is beautiful."

He threw a seed at the woman's head, and she said, "Something hurts." She removed her scalp, laid it across her lap, and picked out a louse.

"Ah!" said Nuxi. "This woman must be the daughter of Death Maker." And he threw another seed at her bare skull. It hurt.

"This hurts very much!" cried the daughter of Death Maker. "You parrot! You're hurting my head." And again he struck her naked skull. She put her scalp back on, got up, and continued walking. Then she pushed aside the lid to her cave, and her head disappeared in the earth.

The daughter of Death Maker went in first. The mole catcher went after her. Inside he managed to find the path, although it was very dark. After he had walked a short distance, he came into the light again. When he had walked ten paces, a brightness appeared. The sun had come out. "It's dawn!" he said.

In half an hour he reached the house of Sukunkyum, the elder brother of Our Lord. He went inside, and they gave him corn soup. They hid him there. "We mustn't let Death Maker eat you, mole catcher," said Our Lady, the wife of Sukunkyum. She took a kettle and put it over him. He kept himself hidden there. It was she who hid him. She toasted chilis and ground them up, then she sprinkled them on his back.

After a while Death Maker arrived. Our Lady, the wife of Sukunkyum, said, "Come in, Death Maker." And the

moment he entered, he smelled a man. "What could that odor be? I smell something good to eat."

"You don't smell anything," said Our Lady.

He detected the odor of Nuxi, but he also smelled the chili. "Horrible! What a horrible odor!" cried Death Maker, and he sneezed. "Horrible, I'm leaving!"

In a while he came back. "Great Lady," he called, "I've come to see you."

"Sukunkyum isn't here," said Our Lady. "What do you want?"

"Nothing," said Death Maker. "I just wanted to pay you a visit." But the wife of Sukunkyum was becoming annoyed. So Death Maker went away.

At last the elder brother of Our Lord came in with the sun on his shoulders. He gave the sun its supper. The sun ate beans and tortillas, and sardines with squash seeds.

"I'm thirsty," said Sukunkyum, and Our Lady gave him a drink. Then the great lady said to him, "One of my children has come here, not a dead man but one who is still living."

"Let me see him," replied Sukunkyum. The great lady showed him what was under the kettle.

"Take care of him for me," said Sukunkyum. "Don't

let Death Maker eat him. I have to go now. I'll see him when I come back. It won't be long." And when Sukunkyum had finished eating, he set out to place the sun at the foot of the sky.

Toward evening he returned and had his supper, and afterward he showed Nuxi some old clothes that he had. "Put on these," he said, and he gave them to him.

"Very well," said Nuxi, and he put them on.

When it became light again, Sukunkyum said, "Go wash your clothes now. I'll show you where the water is, mole catcher." And he showed him. "It's right over there," he said. "That's where you have to go. Death Maker won't find you. He never passes that way." Then he gave him chili, ashes, and lime, and he went off to do his washing. He washed the clothes three times with the chili, the ashes, and the lime, returning at noon to the house of the elder brother of Our Lord.

"So there you are!" said Sukunkyum. "Now get to work and cut firewood." And the ancient one began to do the work, so that he would be able to take his supper with the elder brother of Our Lord. "Death Maker won't eat you now," said Sukunkyum. "You can go wherever you like, all day long. Death Maker won't do anything to you."

Just then the daughter of Death Maker arrived. Sukunkyum turned to Nuxi and asked, "Is she the one who brought you here?"

"Yes," he replied.

"Come in, then, and grind corn. Come in and work," said Sukunkyum. "Make food for my son."

"I will not serve him," said the young woman.

Sukunkyum became angry. "You will serve him right now," he ordered. "Serve him! You are the one who brought him here."

"Very well," she said, and she came in and began to work. She made all the tortillas and the corn soup.

"She belongs to you," said Sukunkyum to the ancient one. "She brought you here."

"Yes," said Nuxi, "and I will go be with her in the house of Death Maker."

Sukunkyum gave the mole catcher his clothes, and he put them on. "Go now to the house of Death Maker."

"But won't he eat me?"

"No," said Sukunkyum, "because you will change yourself into a little bird." He gave him the feathers, and he put them on. When the mole catcher reached the house of Death Maker, he was no longer a man but a bird.

"What little bird is this?" said Death Maker, and he shot a small arrow that stunned the bird, and it dropped to the ground. Death Maker's daughter got up and caught the bird, thinking to keep it as a pet.

"You're not going to let it live," said Death Maker. "Kill it, so I can eat it."

"I will not kill it," she said. "It belongs to me."

"My bad daughter refuses to kill it!" And as she ran off with it, he chased her.

"His hummingbird is my pet!" she cried. "My pet hummingbird!" Death Maker did not know it was Nuxi. All he could see was a little bird.

When she got back to the house, she kept the bird hidden inside her tunic. That night the bird became a man again. Her father knew nothing about it. Then she said to Nuxi, "My father will discover us any moment—my father and mother both."

"You are right," said Nuxi.

She got up and called to her parents. No sooner had she told them than Death Maker acted sick. He vomited. Then his wife vomited, and when all the vomiting was finished, Death Maker screamed at his daughter, "Show me my son-in-law!"

"Here he is," she replied.

"Light the fire," he said. "Give me light so I can see him. I want to see what he looks like."

She went over and lit the fire, and as the light fell on Nuxi, her father saw that he was blue, all dressed in blue. "Are you my daughter's husband?" cried Death Maker.

"I am," replied Nuxi.

Then Death Maker was content. "Tomorrow you will cut my firewood."

"Very well," said Nuxi, and the next morning he set out to cut wood. "Let's go bring in your father's kindling," he said to his wife.

"There, that's my father's kindling," said the daughter of Death Maker.

"Those aren't sticks, those are bones," said Nuxi. Then he went and cut wood from the *luwin* tree, bundled it up, and carried it to his father-in-law. When they got to the house, they laid it down and built his fire. "Here is your kindling," said Nuxi.

"Excellent!" cried Death Maker. "Now I have my firewood. It's cold!" And he curled up next to the fire.

As soon as Nuxi had finished his work for Death Maker, he went to work for Sukunkyum. He took his meals there, because the food at Death Maker's house was not good.

"Death Maker's food is bad," warned Sukunkyum. "Don't eat it. Have your meals here instead. Death Maker's tortillas are bracket fungi. His beans are not beans but larvae of the green fly. His corn paste isn't corn paste. It's the flesh of your people, the decayed flesh of human beings. Take a little and bring it to me, but be careful not to touch it with your hand. It stinks horribly."

"I'll bring you some," said Nuxi, and he did.

"Tomorrow I'll show you what this food really is," said Sukunkyum. "Death Maker makes you think you're seeing beans, but tomorrow you'll see that they've turned into larvae. Tomorrow you'll see his tortillas are fungi. You'll see that this corn paste is the decayed flesh of your people."

At noon Sukunkyum sat down to his meal. He said to Nuxi, "Go get Death Maker's daughter, and bring her here to eat."

Sukunkyum and Nuxi went together to see Death Maker. When they got to his house, Sukunkyum gave the order: "It would be good if your daughter came and ate at my house with my son."

"Very well," replied Death Maker, and he said to his daughter, "Go. Go eat with my son-in-law, Nuxi." Then Nuxi and his wife returned with the elder brother of Our Lord.

Sukunkyum sat down with Nuxi, and they ate together, while the daughter of Death Maker sat down to eat with the wife of Sukunkyum. The great lady said to her, "This is a real tortilla. You must eat it."

"It is not good," she said. "I cannot eat with you, great lady."

"Eat it!" cried the lady. "It was you who brought the mole catcher here."

"Eat it!" cried Sukunkyum. "It was you who brought me my son, who is now your husband."

"Eat it!" cried Nuxi. "You are my wife!"

"Very well," said the daughter of Death Maker, and she ate with the lady.

Lacandon

How the Christ Child Was Warmed

"Won't you give me a place for the night?" said Joseph. He walked and walked. The Christ Child was about to be born.

"No, there's no place to sleep. Go take a walk, beggar!" he was told. He went to another town. "Won't you please give me a place for the night, because my wife is sick," said Joseph.

"Oh, there's no place to sleep. If you want, you can go to the stable," said the owner.

"All right, if you would be so kind, even if it's a stable, because my wife's baby will be born tonight," he said.

"All right, then," said the owner. They went to the stable. The Christ Child was born. A very heavy frost fell. The Christ Child was dying of the cold.

The cow was good-hearted. She breathed on the baby. The Christ Child was revived. He was dying of the cold. The cow warmed the baby with her breath. She blew and blew on the baby. That's how the Christ Child was warmed. Our Lord didn't die of the cold. When morning came he already had a halo around his head. It was revealed that he was Our Lord.

Tzotzil

How Christ Was Chased

When Jesus Christ was a prisoner, they thought he was smoking in jail. They thought they saw the end of his lighted cigar. But it was not he, it was the firefly, and Jesus Christ had already fled.

He came to a river and crossed over. But as he was crossing the river, he stepped on fresh-water snails. When the ones who were chasing him reached the river's edge and could not see which way he had gone, they questioned the snails. The snails replied, "Don't you see that he has trampled on us and turned us over?"

The pursuers went on and passed some birds. They

were white-fronted doves. The birds cried, "No way through here, no way through here," and because they had tried to help him, Jesus decreed that, from then on, the white-fronted doves would be able to enter grottoes and water holes and drink whenever they were thirsty.

But the pursuers went ahead and opened a path with their machetes. Then the white-winged dove cried, "There he is among the trees, there he is among the trees." Jesus Christ had already gone, but because the white-winged dove had tried to betray him, he decreed that, from then on, it would not be able to enter grottoes and water holes.

Jesus hid under some banana trees. "That's him, he's near now," said the ones who were chasing him. The magpie-jay was there. He was a human once. "Is it Our Lord you're looking for? He's here," said the magpie-jay. "Seize him! He's here now." Then they captured Our Lord. They made him carry a cross.

Toad and Hawk

There's a story about the toad and the hawk. They say
that one day the hawk decided to go where Our Father
is, in the sky. Well, he met the toad, and he said, "I'm
going walking up above, where God is." The hawk and
the toad, they say, were good friends.

"I want to go with you," said Toad to his friend.

"You, you can't go!" said Hawk. But the toad began
eyeing his friend's bag. He jumped in and lay down inside. And when hawk was ready to go, Toad was in the
bag.

When Hawk arrived in the sky, Toad jumped out, came
around, and greeted his friend.

"When did you come here?" asked Hawk.

"I came before you," said Toad.

"But, friend, how did you get here?"

"Oh, I just came. I came before you. I've been here awhile."

But when the hawk flew back to earth, the toad stayed up above. There was no way for him to return. The hawk, with his wings, just floated down to the ground.

Not knowing how to come back, the toad kept looking at the earth. He said to himself, "Maybe I can do the same."

So he let himself go, and he floated in the sky. But when he hit the earth, he flattened out. He landed hard, and his belly spread out wide.

That's why the toad today has a big belly. It's where he hit himself when he fell, they say, because he was not carried down by his friend. He was left behind.

But I was not standing there looking when he fell to earth. If I had been there, I would have caught him in my hat.

Chorti

The Monkey's Haircut

It seems there was a monkey living in the house of a rich gentleman, and whatever anybody did he would watch, to see if he could do it, too. That way he was learning all the time.

One day, while he was sweeping inside the house, he saw his master having a haircut and a shave and all the extras. Well, he began to feel like having the same himself. "Why not a haircut for me, too?" he thought.

Then he began to sweep seriously. He just did sweeping, and before he knew it he had swept up a centavo. "Now there's a start," he said, "toward the whole price of my haircut."

The next day he was sweeping again, and all at once he swept up a five-centavo piece. "Now I'm really getting there," he said.

The day after that he found another five centavos. "Just one more for my haircut," he said. He had eleven now, and the hair cut cost twelve.

The following day he swept up one last centavo, and without wasting time he ran off to the house where the barber was. "Señor," he called, "cut my hair, please."

"But . . . but . . ." said the barber, "but . . . why not? Get up in this chair and sit still." So the monkey got into the chair, and the haircut began.

Well, it began with a little combing to start off with. Well, the barber tried to use the comb, but then he said, "Monkey, what's there to cut on this head? It's bald. Is this possible?" The barber rubs this way and that way on the monkey's head, but he can't find the hair. There isn't any. "So now what?" he says.

"Well," said the monkey, "if there isn't any, just shave my tail."

The barber picked up the tail and went to work on it, shaving it nice and clean. When it was completely shaved and everything was finished, he said, "Now you're all set." Then the monkey paid him and ran out the door and down the street—with the tail standing up behind him like a tall white candle.

But after he had gone a block, he thought of something. "Oh," he said, "I forgot to get my hair clippings," because he remembered that his master had had the clippings swept up and taken out of the room. Back he ran to the barber. "Give me my hair," he said. "I forgot to take it."

"But, monkey," said the barber, "why didn't you tell me? Now it's all mixed up with everybody else's."

"Give it to me or I'll take your razor," said the monkey, and he snatched the razor and tore off down the street.

Next thing he knew, he was running alongside the butcher's shop, and inside, the butcher was working with a dull old knife. The monkey could hear him saying, "Oh, this knife!"

"Señor," said the monkey, "how about this one?" and he showed him the razor. "Here, try it out!"

"But I'm afraid it would break," said the butcher.

"Don't worry," said the monkey. "If it breaks, it breaks."

"Let's have it, then!"

So he left it with him, saying, "I'll come back for it in

the afternoon when you're through with your work."
Then he ran home to his master's and did who knows
what until it was time to go back to the butcher's again.
And now he's off, running back for the razor. "Where is
it?"

"But, monkey," said the butcher, "I told you it was
going to break, and I was right. It broke."

"Then I'll take your guitar," said the monkey. He
snatched the butcher's guitar and ran down the street,
around a corner, and down another street. He came to a
gate in a neighborhood wall, an old mud wall, and he
climbed up over the gate, sat down, and began to sing
and play the guitar:

> chinki churinki
> shortening bread
> and a big big
> big guitar

But the butcher had run along behind him, and now
he, too, was on the wall, singing:

> devil
> will get you
> he's got you
> monkey

"What's it to you?" called the monkey.

> devil
>
> will get you
>
> he's got you
>
> monkey

"What's it to you?" And the monkey kept on:

> chinki churinki
>
> shortening bread
>
> and a big big
>
> big guitar

And with that the old wall suddenly caved in, burying the poor monkey beneath it.

But the last time I passed by, they were breaking it all up. So I think it's possible they'll get him out yet.

Yucatec

Notes on Sources and Variants

Sources are here given by author or by author and short title. Type numbers from Aarne and Thompson and motif numbers from S. Thompson are assigned to those stories that appear to have been imported from Europe or Africa. For full titles of works cited, see Bibliography.

Introduction

Page 3/two Maya riddles: Andrade, p. 1648; Roys, p. 127. Page 9/Tzotzil conversation between coparents: Laughlin, *Of Shoes,* p.162. Page 10/corn addressed as "divine grace" or "Our Lord's sunbeams": Redfield and Villa Rojas, p. 45; Laughlin, *Of Cabbages,* p. 335. Page 12/recent Lacandon information: Bruce. Page 13/the translation Green Sun: Thompson, *Maya History,* p. 361. Page 13/Juan Tul described: Barrera Vázquez, p.

· 144

12. Page 14/ejemplo and cuento: R. Redfield, p. 292; M. P. Redfield, p. 4; Burns, pp. 19–24. Page 18/*Popol Vuh* stories of hero and grandmother, death's-head in underworld, and firefly cigar: Tedlock, pp. 119–30, 114–17, and 137. Page 19/firefly shown on Maya jar: Coe, *Maya Scribe*, p. 99. page 20/story told by Bernardino Tun: Andrade, p. 57.

Stories

Page 25/The Bird Bride (Yucatec). Freely translated from the Spanish in Barrera Vázquez, p. 25. Aarne-Thompson type 550, *Search for the Golden Bird*.

Page 32/The Miser's Jar (Kekchi). Adapted from Gordon, p. 134. Similar to Aarne-Thompson types 1536B, *The Three Hunchback Brothers Drowned*, and 1730, *The Entrapped Suitors*. Compare Rael, nos. 42–45.

Page 37/Buzzard Man (Tzotzil). A composite drawn from three versions translated by Robert M. Laughlin, in Laughlin, *Of Cabbages*, pp. 50, 246, and 342. Maya variants: AGUACATEC, CAKCHIQUEL, MAM, TZOTZIL, TZUTUHIL—see Laughlin, *Of Cabbages*, p. 51. Also: KEKCHI—Furbee-Losee, vol. 1, p. 30; TZUTUHIL—Orellana, p. 856.

Page 44/Tup and the Ants (Yucatec). Adapted from J. E. S. Thompson, *Ethnology*, p. 163.

Page 52/The Corn in the Rock. A composite drawn mainly from the Kekchi version in Burkitt, pp. 211–25, with details added from these variants: IXIL—Furbee-Losee, vol. 3, p. 65; KEKCHI—J. E. S. Thompson, *Ethnology*, p. 134; MAM—Furbee-Losee, vol. 1, pp. 95–96; TZELTAL—Slocum, p. 2. Other Maya variants: CAKCHIQUEL, MAM, POKOMCHI, TZELTAL, YUCATEC—see J. E. S. Thompson, *Maya History*, pp. 348–54. Also: QUICHE—Shaw, p. 41; MAM—Furbee-Losee, vol. 1, p. 95; POKOMCHI—Mayers, pp. 6 and 12, Shaw, p. 207; TZELTAL—Nash, pp. 43, 44, and 326–27.

Page 56/Rosalie (Yucatec). Adapted from J. E. S. Thompson, *Ethnology*, p. 167. Maya variants: JACALTEC—Shaw, p. 131; YUCATEC—J. E. S. Thompson, *Ethnology*, p. 175. Aarne-Thompson type 313, *The Girl as Helper in the Hero's Flight*. Rael, no. 144.

Page 66/Chac (Yucatec). Adapted from J. E. S. Thompson, *Ethnology*, p. 146. The story The Lord of the Clouds, immediately following, is a Mam variant. For another Yucatec variant, see Andrade, p. 1.

Page 70/The Lord of the Clouds (Mam). Translated from the Spanish in Morales, p. 10. For variants, see preceding note.

Page 72/Rabbit and Coyote (Mam-Kekchi). Translated from the Spanish in Morales, p. 3, with details added from J. E. S. Thompson, *Ethnology*, p. 178. Variants of the episodes included in this tale and in Rabbit and Puma: CAKCHIQUEL—R. Redfield, p. 56; CHUJ—Shaw, p. 105; KEKCHI—Gordon, p. 143; LACANDON—Baer, p. 268; POCOMAM—Furbee-Losee, vol. 1, p. 86; TZELTAL—Trujillo Maldonado, p. 167; TZOTZIL—Laughlin, *Of Cabbages*, pp. 31, 66, 159, 323, and 367. See also sources listed for Rabbit and Puma, below. Aarne-Thompson types 175, *The Tarbaby and the Rabbit*, and 34B, *Wolf Drinks Water to Get Cheese*. S. Thompson motifs K 842.3, "Tied animal persuades another to take his place," and K 1035, "Stone (hard fruit) thrown into greedy dupe's mouth."

Page 77/Rabbit and Puma (Yucatec-Tzutuhil). A composite drawn from three Yucatec sources—Andrade, p. 89, Rosado Vega, p. 192, J. E. S. Thompson, *Ethnology*, p. 179—and a Tzutuhil variant in Orellana, p. 852. See variants listed for Rabbit and Coyote, above. Aarne-Thompson type 1530, *Holding up the Rock*. S. Thompson motif K 1023.5, "Dupe induced to strike at bee's (wasp's) nest."

Page 81/Rabbit Gets Married (Kanhobal). Adapted from the Spanish in Diego Antonio and Dakin. Maya variant: TOJOLABAL—Furbee-Losee, vol. 3, p. 116. S. Thompson motif K 1384, "Female overpowered when caught in tree cleft (hole in hedge)."

Page 84/Lord Sun's Bride (Kekchi). Composite drawn from Dieseldorff, pp. 4–5, J. E. S. Thompson, *Ethnology*, pp. 126–29, and Gordon, pp. 120–21. Other Maya variants: CAKCHIQUEL—R. Redfield, p. 291; IXIL—Furbee-Losee, vol. 3, p. 60; MOPAN—Shaw, p. 176; POKOMCHI—Mayers, p. 3.

Page 92/The Lost Children (Kekchi). Translated from the Spanish in Goubaud Carrera, p. 119. Aarne-Thompson type 327, *The Children and the Ogre.*

Page 94/The Bad Compadre (Cakchiquel). Adapted from R. Redfield, p. 243. Similar, in part, to Aarne-Thompson type 531, *Ferdinand the True and Ferdinand the False.* S. Thompson motifs H 1091.1, "Task: sorting grains: performed by helpful ants," and H 1133.1, "Task: building magic castle."

Page 107/Blue Sun (Tzeltal). Adapted from Slocum, p. 7. Full variants: CHOL—see J. E. S. Thompson, *Maya History*, p. 362; TZOTZIL—Guiteras-Holmes, p. 183. Other Maya variants: CAKCHIQUEL, KANHOBAL, KEKCHI, QUICHE—see J. E. S. Thompson, *Maya History*, pp. 360–62. Also: CHUJ—Shaw, p. 101.

Page 113/The Charcoal Cruncher (Tzotzil). A composite drawn from five versions translated by Robert M. Laughlin, in Laughlin, *Of Cabbages*, pp. 65, 178, 301, 333, and 372. Other Maya variants: KEKCHI—J. E. S. Thompson, *Ethnology*, p. 158; TZOTZIL—Laughlin, *Of Cabbages*, p. 320.

Page 118/How a Witch Escaped (Kekchi). Adapted from Gordon, p. 124.

Page 121/The Mole Catcher (Lacandon). Translated from the Spanish in Bruce, p. 224.

Page 131/How the Christ Child Was Warmed (Tzotzil). English version by Robert M. Laughlin, in Laughlin, *Of Cabbages*, p. 331. Maya variants: KANHOBAL—Siegel, p. 121; YUCATEC—M. P. Redfield, p. 25.

Page 133/How Christ Was Chased. This five-paragraph version has the following sources: first paragraph, CAKCHIQUEL—R. Redfield, p. 65; second paragraph, KEKCHI—J. E. S. Thompson, *Ethnology*, p. 161; third and fourth paragraphs, YUCATEC—M. P. Redfield, p. 13, Rosado Vega, p. 163; fifth paragraph, TZOTZIL—Laughlin, *Of Cabbages*, p. 26. Other Maya tales of the pursuit of Christ: HUASTEC, KANHOBAL QUICHE, TZOTZIL, TZUTUHIL—see Laughlin, *Of Cabbages*, p. 335. Also: IXIL—Shaw, p. 114; TZOTZIL—Gossen, p. 337, Laughlin, *Of Cabbages*, pp. 334, 336, and 384; YUCATEC—Andrade, pp. 545–56, M. P. Redfield, p. 11. Presumed Old World sources going back to the thirteenth century are mentioned in Laughlin, *Of Cabbages*, p. 335.

Page 136/Toad and Hawk (Chorti). Adapted from Fought, p. 144. Maya variant: POCOMAM—Shaw, p. 195. S. Thompson motifs *A 2214.7, "Ancient toad's jump down from heaven accounts for flat body," and *J 512.16, "Toad tries to fly back from heaven like falcon, but is smashed flat."

Page 138/The Monkey's Haircut (Yucatec). Adapted from Vermont-Salas, no. 4; Norman McQuown in Furbee-Losee, vol. 2, p. 55; and Andrade, p. 33. Similar to Aarne-Thompson type 1655, *The Profitable Exchange*. Compare Rael, no. 47.

Bibliography

The abbreviation MCMCA stands for Microfilm Collection of Manuscripts on Cultural Anthropology, a series distributed by the Joseph Regenstein Library, University of Chicago.

Aarne, Antti, and Stith Thompson. *The Types of the Folktale: A Classification and Bibliography*, Folklore Fellows Communications, no. 184. Helsinki: Suomalainen Tiedeakatemia, 1973.

Andrade, Manuel J. "Yucatec Maya Stories," MCMCA, no. 262, 1977.

Baer, Mary E. "The Rabbit and Mountain Lion," *Tlalocan*, vol. 6 (1970), pp. 268–75. Mexico.

Barrera Vázquez, Alfredo. *Recopilación de cuentos mayas*, Colección "Lunes," no. 29. Mexico, 1947.

Bruce, Robert D. *El libro de Chan K'in*, Colección Científica (lingüística), no. 12. Mexico: Instituto Nacional de Antropología e Historia, 1974.

Burkitt, Robert. *The Hills and the Corn: A Legend of the Kekchí Indians of Guatemala . . .* , Anthropological Publications of the University Museum, vol. 8, no. 2. Philadelphia: University of Pennsylvania, 1920.

Burns, Allan F. *An Epoch of Miracles: Oral Literature of the Yucatec Maya.* Austin: University of Texas Press, 1983.

Coe, Michael D. *Lords of the Underworld: Masterpieces of Maya Ceramics.* Princeton, N.J.: Princeton University Press, 1978.

———. *The Maya Scribe and His World.* New York: Grolier Club, 1973.

Diego Antonio, Diego de, and Karen Dakin. "El conejo y la coyota," *Tlalocan*, vol. 9 (1982), pp. 161–72. Mexico.

Dieseldorff, E. P. *Kunst und Religion der Mayavölker.* Berlin: Julius Springer, 1926.

Espinosa, Aurelio M. *Cuentos populares españoles.* 3 vols. Madrid, 1946.

Fought, John G. *Chorti (Mayan) Texts 1.* Philadelphia: University of Pennsylvania Press, 1972.

Furbee-Losee, Louanna, ed. *Mayan Texts*, 3 vols. Chicago: University of Chicago Press, 1976–80.

Gordon, G. B. "Guatemala Myths," *Museum Journal*, vol. 6 (1915), pp. 103–44. University of Pennsylvania.

Gossen, Gary H. *Chamulas in the World of the Sun.* Cambridge: Harvard University Press, 1974.

Goubaud Carrera, Antonio. "Notes on San Juan Chamelco, Alta Verapaz," MCMCA, no. 23, 1949.

Guiteras-Holmes, C[alixta]. *Perils of the Soul: The World View of a Tzotzil Indian.* New York: Free Press of Glencoe, 1961.

Laughlin, Robert M. *Of Cabbages and Kings: Tales from Zinacantán*, Smithsonian Contributions to Anthropology, no. 23, 1977.

———. *Of Shoes and Ships and Sealing Wax: Sundries from Zinacantán*, Smithsonian Contributions to Anthropology, no. 25, 1980.

Mayers, Marvin, *Pocomchi Texts.* Norman, Okla.: Summer Institute of Linguistics of the University of Oklahoma, 1958.

Morales, Pablo. "Cuentos mames" (tr. Norman A. McQuown), MCMCA, no. 130, 1977.

Nash, June. *In the Eyes of the Ancestors: Belief and Behavior in a Maya Community*. New Haven: Yale University Press, 1970.

Orellana, Sandra L. "Folk Literature of the Tzutujil Maya," *Anthropos*, vol. 70 (1975), pp. 839–76. Anthropos Institute, Mödling, Austria.

Rael, Juan B. *Cuentos españoles de Colorado y Nuevo México*. 2d. ed. rev. 2 vols. Santa Fe: Museum of New Mexico Press, 1977.

Redfield, Margaret Park. "The Folk Literature of a Yucatecan Town," *Contributions to American Archaeology*, no. 13, Carnegie Institution of Washington, 1935.

Redfield, Robert. "Notes on San Antonio Palopo," MCMCA, no. 4, 1945.

Redfield, Robert, and Alfonso Villa Rojas. *Chan Kom: A Maya Village*. Chicago: University of Chicago Press, 1962.

Rosado Vega, Luis. *El alma misteriosa del Mayab*. Mexico: Ediciones Botas, 1957.

Roys, Ralph L. *The Book of Chilam Balam of Chumayel*. Norman: University of Oklahoma Press, 1967.

Shaw, Mary, ed. *According to Our Ancestors: Folk Texts from Guatemala and Honduras*. Guatemala: Instituto Lingüístico de Verano, 1971.

Siegel, Morris. "The Creation Myth and Acculturation in Acatán, Guatemala," *Journal of American Folklore*, vol. 56 (1943), pp. 120–26.

Slocum, Marianna C. "The Origin of Corn and Other Tzeltal Myths," *Tlalocan*, vol. 5 (1965), pp. 1–45. Mexico.

Tedlock, Dennis. *Popol Vuh*. New York: Simon and Schuster, 1985.

Thompson, J. Eric. S. *Ethnology of the Mayas of Southern and Central British Honduras*, Anthropological Series, vol. 17, no. 2. Chicago: Field Museum of Natural History, 1930.

———. *Maya History and Religion*. Norman: University of Oklahoma Press, 1970.

Thompson, Stith. *Motif-Index of Folk Literature*, 6 vols. Bloomington: University of Indiana Press, 1955–58.

Trujillo Maldonado, Joaquín. "El conejo y el coyote," *Tlalocan*, vol. 8 (1980), pp. 167–77. Mexico.

Vermont-Salas, Refugio, tr. "Yucatec Maya Texts" (collected by Manuel J. Andrade), MCMCA, no. 108, 1971.